Born in 1945, Eugenia Fakino   ...is. She has
written four novels. *The Seventh Gi   * was written in 1983.
A best-seller in Greece, *The Seventh Garment* has been
translated into French, Russian and Hungarian and is the
first of Eugenia Fakinou's novels to be translated into
English.

THE SEVENTH GARMENT

Eugenia Fakinou

Translated by
Ed Emery

Library of Congress Catalog Card Number: 91-61200

British Library Cataloguing in Publication Data
Fakinou, Eugenia
  The seventh garment
  I. Title
  889 (F)

  ISBN 1-85242-186-X

First published in Greece in 1983 as *To Evdhomo Roucho*
Copyright © Eugenia Fakinou & Thanasis Kastaniotis 1983
Translation copyright © Serpent's Tail 1991

This edition first published in 1991 by
Serpent's Tail, 4 Blackstock Mews, London N4 and
401 West Broadway #2, New York, NY 10012

Set 10½/14 Galliard by AKM Associates (UK) Ltd, Southall, London
Printed in Finland by Werner Söderström Oy

The publishers would like to thank George Kolios for his assistance
with Greek historical events and place names.
Publication was partly made possible by financial support from
The Hellenic Foundation, and the Commission of the European
Communities, Brussels.

THE TREE

I love women. Women and wild flowers. I love the colours of wild flowers. White, yellow and purple. These are the colours of the land. In ancient times people painted their statues those colours, and in later times they painted their doors and window frames the same. People don't paint their doors and windows frames any more. Those are the colours of crocuses and anemones, lilies, irises and asphodel. White, yellow, and purple.

Women are suffering greatly again. It is women who write History. They carry the world's great events on their shoulders.

In the old days, the maidens from the distant North would come, and we would talk together. Then came the priestesses, clad in white, with their copper gongs, and garlands in their hair. In their white robes they would lie down and wait and listen for the whispering of my leaves.

They would ask me of things both great and small. And I would tell them. Because I knew. The birds from Libya used to tell me; and the snakes from Acherousia; and the Sun, the great lover; and the invisible flowers; and the far-off stars and constellations.

ROULA

My mother always used to say that you can tell a bad day from the way it starts. Well, she wasn't wrong. And now I've got this jerk rubbing himself up against me. Who do you think you are? God's gift to the world? Here – try this for size . . . a quick elbow in the ribs. Nice one! That's got rid of him. That's the only way to deal with them. In the old days, when I was a kid, I used to be very ladylike about it. I'd say: 'Excuse me sir . . . do you mind . . .!' Fucking 'sir' indeed . . .! And he'd start protesting how he couldn't help it, because the bus was so packed, and if he'd really meant to do it he'd have found someone better-looking. So in the end I stopped playing their game. A good jab with my elbow, give them something to squeal about, and I stare innocently out of the window. Anyway, I already know what's in store for us today. Thursday. The usual programme. We'll all have to troop into the boss's office, and he'll have chairs arranged for us, around his desk. He'll have the layout proofs of yesterday's magazine in his hands, and he'll have been up half the night marking our mistakes with a red marker pen. Stupid little things. 'You made a mistake with Scrooge's sleeves. You've done one of them green and the other one blue.' (What the hell do the kids care if Scrooge's got one sleeve green and the other one blue?! As if they'd even notice . . .!) 'The caption's in the wrong place; where it says "will", that was meant to go underneath.' 'A lot of the squares weren't filled in, in the crossword.' 'Roula, you're still doing the skies blue. . .' (How the hell do you want them – yellow?!!) 'They need a little mauve, and a slightly lighter blue – about 10 per cent.' What a load of crap! He'll keep us there for half an hour, so he can have a good moan. 'You're all smoking too much. Especially you, Roula. (I bet he's counting them.) And all I ever see is you lot stuffing yourselves with sandwiches and cups of coffee. You mess around all morning, and then when you realize that you haven't enough time to finish your schedules, you just bang the films out any old how, so as to get them done by lunchtime.' You know what I think? To hell with the lot of them. Scrooge especially. . . And as for Goofy. . . I mean, it's hardly the end of the world, is it!

Ah, here we go. The old bastard's started again. I know what, I'll stand on his foot. Nice and hard. That should shut him up. You know, they really get on my nerves – especially since I'm still in a strange sort of mood after last night.

It was odd, that. I don't usually have dreams. Mind you, when I say that to the others in the office, they laugh. 'You *do* dream.' they say. 'It's just that you don't remember them.' Anyway, last night I had a dream.

The Dream

I dreamt that I was living a long way from the city. It wasn't somewhere I knew; but I felt somehow at home there. I was sleeping with some other girls in a room. Maybe they were my sisters, who knows. . . All of a sudden – help! There was an earthquake. I rushed outside, just in time to see the roof of the house come crashing down. Only one pillar of the house was left standing. And in my dreams it started sprouting golden hair, and speaking in a man's voice. Bizarre, even for a dream. Because the pillar of a house is supposed to be the man. And it's weird for a thing like a column to start growing blond hair and talking. Let alone the fact that I don't even have a home like that. We've always lived in rented flats. And there aren't any men in my family. No family, either, come to that. My father died when I was a kid, and my mother died four years ago. She had family back in the village, but I knew nothing about them. I'm not married, and I've got no boyfriend (not at the moment, anyway. . .). So who can the man have been? I told the girls in the office about it this morning. Mitsa, who knows all about stuff like that, said, 'You're going to get some bad news.' And Olga said: 'It must be a death, somewhere. Far away, out of town.'

Anyway, since there's no men in my life, why should I worry! It can't have anything to do with me. Men, I tell you. . . they give you a hard time all week, and then they even come to haunt your dreams. I still have a few accounts to settle with the male sex. Up till now I've usually put up with it, but the next time I'll give them something to think about. Dirty bastards! Once they've had their leg over, they don't want to know. . . It's all 'I love you', flowers and tenderness, until it – the 'worldly' – happens, and then what? The second time it's just: 'Come on, get your clothes off, let's get on with it.'

When we talk about sex in the office, we call it 'the worldly'. From when they had those priests up on trial for screwing, and the priests said they were only doing 'worldly things' – meaning what 'worldly' people, ordinary people, did. Jenny brought in the newspaper. We were laughing so much the building shook. Imagine it, these priests, with their 'worldlies'! Ever since then, we say 'how was your worldly last night', or 'how many worldlies last week', and nobody else knows what we're talking about. . . It's our private joke. After all, if you can't have a laugh once in a while, how are you going to get through the day? We used to work in the morning and then in the afternoon, with a long lunch break in between, but now they've abolished the lunch break, and the day seems to go on for ever. All those fucking skies to paint. Because that's what I do for a living – colouring skies all day long. There's a girl who's from art college, who writes on the photocopies what percentage yellow, how much blue and how much red to use, and so on, and we just do the colouring. Mind you, it's nice to have the chance to use a bit of colour. . . usually they tell us just to use grey. . . different shades of grey. It saves them money. They knock out the negative, ready for printing, and there's no point imagining romantic skies, with blue and mauve and so on. Everything comes out bloody grey.

Here we are – Rialto. I'll get off at Skyrou Street and go to the socialists at the corner shop for bread and yoghurt. I've had enough of eggs. They'll end up chirping inside me. Let's try a diet yoghurt today. Given this weird mood I'm in, I should try to cook something this afternoon, it'd give me something to do. Either moussaka or pastitsio. Every now and then I feel like making a big pie. It lasts a week, then I get sick of it and start back on the eggs. I get sick of eggs too, so I start on yoghurt or Knorr soups, and, yuk! I'm back where I started. Every now and then I cook for the old lady next door. I call her 'granny'. I love my granny. She's such a survivor. Imagine it – eighty years old, with a pacemaker, and she lives all on her own. *On her own*! She's been living here for as long as I've been in these flats. Since they were built, in fact. Ten years ago. My mum was alive then. Granny – we've always called her that – had a TV, but when that wasn't working she used to get lonely. So she was always knocking at our door with a bit of yoghurt-pie, or a bit of honey. And sometimes we used to go and keep her company. We'd sit and watch TV together. And then when my mum died, Granny helped me get over it. And now I look after her. I do the shopping for her, and in the morning I ring her doorbell to ask what sort of night she's had. . . That kind of thing. And when I cook something she likes, every once in a while, and there's too much for me, I take her a bit next door. We're two women on our own. We've got small studio flats on the inside of the block, but although there's no view from our kitchens, we do get the sun all afternoon. And the rent is pretty cheap. Destoukos has the whole floor, but he doesn't need it all for himself, so he rents out part of it. He's Greek-American, and he gets his pension in dollars. But he's not a bad landlord. He hasn't put our rent up for four years now.

'Hang on, lady – no need to push like that! We're all getting off here. . .!'

Don't look at me like that. . . arsehole! I know what side of the tracks you come from! They look down their noses, as if they're somehow better than us. They're just slags, though. Even if they do wear fur coats in winter. I've decided. I'm going to get myself a good, stylish coat this year, too. I've seen one I fancy – I've as good as put down a deposit already. As Mitsa says, a good coat is an investment. I've made friends with the sales girl in the shop. I told her to keep it for me. She says that I should have bought it in the summer, because it would have been cheaper. How was I supposed to know. . .? I would have saved some money, instead of blowing it all on Hydra.

People were always telling me about Hydra – the discotheques, the cafés, the famous people, and all that, so I kept telling myself: 'Next year I'm going. And this year I did. I tell you, the place is amazing. Ci-vil-iz-ation! People there don't worry about how you behave, how you dress, how you screw, or anything. Doesn't come into it. I had a brilliant time. Got up to all kinds of things. I even got onto someone's yacht. When I told the girls at the office, they were green with envy. Emilia (the one from art school) told me: 'If you don't watch out, you're going to end up in trouble one of these days.' Trouble, indeed! I could tell her what life is – what we eat, what we drink, and whatever we fancy screwing.

'Hi. Two skimmed-milk, low-fat socialist yoghurts, please.'

That's what I say to the socialists down at the corner shop, and it always winds them up. It usually starts a row, and I like that. I don't go in for politics, really. No politician's providing my bread and butter. I got my job thanks to my mum, when she was working as a cleaning lady at the print works. One of the girls from the dark room was off sick, so she gave me the word, and I went along. And thanks to my pussy too, but that's another story. . .

ELENI

These lentils are a torment. They get worse every year. They're half eaten by insects. You go through them, sorting out the bad ones, then you get tired of it and just put them all in the pot anyway. . . But they get worse every year. And we get fewer of them too. We only have about ten kilos these days, and most of them aren't worth eating. The seeds are no good now. . . It's been so many years. . .! Mother brought the seeds with her. She had a petticoat that was all patches. But they weren't patches – they were little pockets that she'd sewn up seeds inside. She had all sorts – chickpeas, beans, black-eyed beans, mint, penny-royal, basil, lentils, buckwheat, beetroot, even flowers. A petticoat full of seeds. Nobody ever knew. Not even that man. And when they threw us out of the big house and we came here, Mother planted her little garden.

She used to say that she had green fingers, and that was why everything grew so well. Mother's garden was the talk of the village. People round here had never seen anything like it. They all used to grow wheat, barley and rye, and that was that. But we had tomatoes, and cucumbers, and all kinds of pumpkins and melons. And Mother was amazing at preserving them all. Some of the vegetables she would dry, and some she would pickle. Could the villagers have done that sort of thing? No. . . But they didn't come asking her for seeds. For them she was always a foreigner, and. . . He left her unmarried till the end. . . And when the villagers heard the story, they wouldn't even come near us. It was as if we had the plague. 'It's better this way,' mother used to say. 'At least this way we stay clean.'

But at school. . . they used to call us bastard this and bastard that. My brother Fotos and I went to school. The others didn't want to. But we dropped out in the fourth year. There was too much work at home.

I'll heat Fotos's soup for him. Three days I've been heating it now, but he won't even open his mouth to taste it. Our Fotos is going – I can see it. Slowly, slowly, he's going. No obvious sickness, no fever, nothing. . . Mother says it's remorse. 'He has a sin within him, and it's consuming him. He's struggled with it all these years, and he's kept it down. But now, as he gets weaker, it's getting the upper hand.' I've done everything for him. I rubbed him with prayer oil. Ever since he fell ill I've been fasting, I haven't washed, and I've been sleeping on the floor. All in vain.

Mother did what she could, but she couldn't do much. I feel sorry for Mother. She lost her sight last year, and she doesn't find it easy to cope. But it's as if her brain is becoming sharper as she loses her physical powers. Her mind seems to take her where it wants. Sometimes to Vourla, the town she came from in Asia Minor, and sometimes to Kavala, or

Chios. And every time a door opens in the house, she asks, 'Is that Persephone. . .?'

There – he jumped up again. And all the lentils scattered as I tried to hold him down. Oh well, I'll just have to pick them up and sort them all over again. . . He doesn't know what he's doing. . . He gets up and starts yelling through gritted teeth . . . He's struggling with someone. . . I try to hold him down as best I can, but it's as if his illness actually gives him strength. He hits me all over. The day before yesterday he gave me a black eye. I was ashamed in case my brothers and sisters came and saw me. But they didn't. Tassos is busy, Thodoroula only comes once in a while, Archontoula is in Athens, and Despo is in Larisa. Fotos and I are bound together forever. We were twins. First Fotos came out, and then me. The priest didn't want to baptize us because we were bastards, but Mother glared at him and said: 'Would you add sin upon sin'. In other words, 'Must the Scripture be fulfilled, that the sins of the fathers be visited upon the children. . .' So he ended up baptizing us. . . not because of the Scripture, but because of the look that Mother gave him. People used to be scared of Mother in those days. . . They used to call her a witch behind her back.

'Stop it, Fotos. Try not to be so agitated. Do you want a little soup. . .? Don't get up, my love. Is it water you want. . .?'

He'll only drink water. As if he's a water snake. As if he's trying to put out the fire that's burning him up. I always keep a jug of fresh water by his bed. Two glasses he drank. Then he fell back on the bed, hardly breathing. He looked like a statue. I don't want to say 'dead' – it would be a bad omen. His hair is completely blond, even though he's getting on for sixty – fifty-eight, to be exact. Mine was black to start with, but it's been grey for many years now. Mother is blonde too. She must be eighty-three this year, since she says she was born in 1900. She doesn't show her years, though. Her hair's so blonde, and her eyes are so clear. Her hearing's very good too – I mean, it always was, and then when she lost her sight she had to rely on her hearing and her sense of smell. But the way her bright eyes move when she talks to you, you'd swear she can see everything. In fact I'm convinced she really *does* see everything. She seems to know everything that's going on. And her sense of touch is wonderful. Her hands are all wrinkled and calloused from working and digging all her life, but when she touches something, she knows what it is, right away. Not just easy things – difficult things, too. 'This bobbin,' she says, 'is black.' Or, 'These beans are no good, they're full of insects.' Or, 'Is that wool you're knitting with blue, Eleni?' (Why does she bother asking, since she already knows?)

Once or twice I've thought that she's lying when she says she can't see. So she can find out whether we're telling her the truth. But Mother would never do a thing like that. And anyway, you can see how it torments her.

I've gathered up the lentils as best I can. I'll have to sweep the rest. I'll do it now that Fotos has quietened down. Only the two of us – the twins – and Archontoula have Mother's looks. Tassos, Yannis, Thodoroula, Despo and poor Spyridoula all look like *him*. Physically, though, we all have Mother's build. She was both mother and father to us, right from the start. *He* only remembered our little cabin when he needed a woman.

He would come in shouting: 'Out, you little bastards,' and even if it was raining or snowing he would throw us out of the room so that he could fulfil his desire, like an animal.

Our little cabin only had one room. Long and narrow, it was. We cooked and slept in the same room. That's where

Mother used to wash herself *afterwards*, in cold water, which was all we had. She had a brush, and she would soap herself and rub and scrub, to get the smell of *him* off her. One time – I must have been about eighteen, because Spyridoula had only just been born – he came into the house again. He shouted at us to get out. All the children went out except the baby and me. I had a fever and was fast asleep, wrapped up in a blanket. I was woken up suddenly by his groaning and heaving. The filthy things he was saying to Mother were terrible to hear. He was hitting her and swearing at her, and Mother was stopping her ears with her hands and she covered her mouth to stop herself screaming. I turned to stone as I watched. And that was the time, the first time, that *it* got a grip on me. I jumped up and started screaming and tearing my nightdress. I was trying to get my hands on him, but I couldn't. Mother threw him off her and got up. She mopped my sweating brow and wiped the froth from my mouth. I was thrashing about like a mad woman, and my arms and legs seemed to have a life of their own. Mother was hugging me and crying. *He* just looked at us without a word. Then he went. I calmed down and fell asleep again. Ever since then *it* has taken me over every once in a while. I feel it coming, and I lie down. I bite on a handkerchief I always carry in my pocket. After a bit it passes. At first I used to be scared. Then I got used to it. My brothers and sisters got used to it too. It doesn't bother us any more. I know what they call me in the village, because it happened to me once outside in the fields, and a villager saw me. 'Moonstruck', they call me. It doesn't bother me, though. . . I don't trouble anyone. . . Later, Mother used to say that it was because of this that I was able to hear prophecies. . . She says: 'The moon tells all, and it's because what it tells you is so terrible that you hit yourself.' If Mother says so, it must be right. And later on, of all my brothers and sisters, I was the only one who could hear the leaves of the oak tree. I was the only one Mother used to take to the Tree with her. I was the one she taught. She told me what she knew. And now she can no longer go, *I* am the only one left who can hear the leaves of the Tree and understand them.

MOTHER

My dear Fotos is up again. He's a torment to the girl. And a torment to himself too, I suppose. I'm losing him, I can feel it. The end is coming, but it will be a while yet. My son will suffer a lot. He will have to pay for all of us. It's unfair – but then life is unfair.

'The servant of God Dimetra and the servant of God Andronikos are now man and wife.'

I liked Andronikos from the moment I first saw him, at my aunt's house. I took him a tray of quinces and pastries. I knew why he was there. That's how things were done in those days. He'd seen me in church and he'd liked the look of me. 'You're a very lucky girl, Dimetra,' my aunt said. 'Because Andronikos is a good man, and good-looking too.'

'I'm not sure about his name, though. . .' I whispered.

'It's a fine name, very fine. Byzantine. And your own name is very old, too. Wasn't that always our custom. . .? so that we never forgot our native land?'

During the wedding celebrations, I was very scared. . . What was going to happen later. . .? All my aunt had told me to expect was 'whatever your husband wants'. His height, and his moustache, scared me. And his name reminded me of grandma's stories about Digenes and his Byzantine soldiers.

But, as my aunt said, I was very lucky. Because Andronikos

had a tannery at Dere, near the Great Bridge. And he could draw too. Saints, icons, Alexander the Great, and so on. He used to draw just for the fun of it. He drew very well. . .! But after – what was going to happen after. . .?

When I found myself alone in the room with him I started crying. Why? I don't even remember, really. But Andronikos took me in his arms like a child and spoke gently to me, as though he were rocking me to sleep. I calmed down and stopped crying. He kissed my tear-filled eyes, and my cheeks. . . And then he stopped. He looked at me as if he was asking my permission, and then he kissed my cheek again, but this time a little lower. . . and a little lower again, until he was kissing the corner of my mouth. And again he stopped. But he didn't take his lips away while he looked at me. I waited. I didn't pull away. Partly because I remembered my aunt's 'whatever your husband wants' and partly because I liked it when Andronikos held me in his arms. . . His lips were still there, at the corner of my mouth. Then he passed like a breath of air across my lips, and then, before I knew where I was, he kissed me properly. I didn't know what I was supposed to do. . .! Should I open my mouth. . .? Should I have my tongue in or out. . .? I was so embarrassed. . .

But Andronikos taught me. . . Gently, and without words.

And as each day dawned, I would think, 'May the whole of our life be like this. . .'

In fact, one day, I whispered it in his ear:

'May the whole of our life be like this. . .'

'And why should it not, my lovely?' he replied, and he stroked me. He used to like to stroke my belly – he loved it, in fact. Simply, gently, round and round.

One day I asked why he did it, and his answer was strange. . .

'It reminds me of a well-ploughed field, which will always bear fruit wherever it is. And the golden tuft of hair that you have, down below, is like corn, ready for the harvest.'

I used to like the way he talked. I wasn't ashamed with him any more.

She's dropped the lentils. Now she'll have to pick them up and sort the clean ones from the dirty ones again.

'Eleni, Eleni. . .! Fotos wants water again.'

My first son. Not my first child, but my first son.

My Persephone was my first child. Born a year after we were married. She was fair-haired and beautiful. We were going to call her Thodora, after Andronikos's late mother, but one evening as I was feeding the child at my breast, Andronikos leapt up. . .

'Persephone! We'll call her Persephone! A Demeter like you, a goddess, can only have had a Persephone as a daughter. . .!'

Andronikos was well-educated. He'd completed secondary school at Vourla. A proper school. He adored the ancient Greeks – Alexander the Great, Theseus, Hercules – but particularly Alexander. He used to draw him, up on his charger, riding among his enemies. He would draw him in the arms of his Roxanne, or loosing the Gordian Knot. If he hadn't been slightly self-conscious, I'm sure he'd have gone round wearing a tunic and a helmet just like the ancients. He was so crazy about the olden days that when they asked him to paint the chapel of St John, he painted the saints so they all looked like ancient Greeks.

One day he brought home some special dyes from the tannery, for drawing patterns on leather – handbags and so on. The dyes came from Vienna, and they were the indelible sort. He decided to dye a little cross on the child's shoulder.

'That way,' he said, laughing, 'if we ever lose her, we'll recognize her when we find her again.'

I was troubled, and made the sign of the cross over the child. I didn't like what he'd said. Andronikos made fun of me. Then, later, he took me aside. I knew what he wanted. He'd been bothering me about it for ages. He'd had this idea. He wanted to draw pictures on my body.

'I'd be ashamed,' I told him. 'The midwife will see it next time I have a baby.'

'And what if she does?' Andronikos laughed. 'She'll only be jealous, because nobody's as beautiful as you – not just because of the drawing. I tell you what – I'll do you the Garden of Eden. Your breasts will be roses, with all kinds of other flowers below them, and on your belly I'll draw a great field of corn, so that it can mingle with your other corn, down there.'

And he wouldn't take no for an answer, no matter how hard I tried to humour him out of it. He drew pictures all over my body with his inks. Nobody else ever saw those drawings. Not the midwife (because I had the rest of my babies on my own, like an animal), and not my children either. Only one other man saw them. *Him*. He was shocked. It stopped him in his tracks. At first he'd thought that I was a prostitute. Afterwards, though, he was frightened. He was scared of the drawings. He used to take me in the dark, with all my clothes on.

A door opened. I'm sure of it. Perhaps it's Persephone?

'Persephone, Persephone. . .? Who's that, Eleni?'

'It's Dimitroula, Mother.'

'Which Dimitroula?'

'Thodoroula's girl.'

'Oh, her. . .' Dimitroula must be nearly thirty by now. She doesn't look like me at all, even if she does have my name. She should take on the mysteries now. My Eleni is getting old. And she's the only unmarried woman we have. When I tell the mysteries, it must be to a virgin.

What's that on the table. . .? Andronikos's head. . .? Yes, yes, that's what it is. Why, Andronikos, my love, why. . .? Why do you still have your eyes open. . .? Close them now, and rest. . . Sixty years have passed since that day. Aren't you tired of having your eyes open so long? What have you come to tell me this time. . .? What have you seen. . .? Have you come to tell us of a death. . .? I know already. . . Everyone has to die, and now it's time for Fotos. But not immediately. He will have to suffer first. You see, he has sin within him. But tell me, my love, why do you only come when you have bad news to bring me. . .? I've wondered about that a lot. . . Is it because you don't want me to be scared by sudden deaths. . .? Is that why you come. . .? My dear, sweet husband. . . I told you, didn't I, but you wouldn't believe me. . . O Andronikos. . .! If only we had left Vourla when I told you. . . we would have escaped. . .! All of us. . .! But you laughed, you called me a coward. Why a coward, my love? Everyone was getting out as fast as they could. And you said: 'It's a squall. It'll pass.' But Aisha, our maid, she told me, Andronikos. She said: 'My people will come for you with knives.' But you, Andronikos, you laughed. It was only when I fell at your knees, and wept, and said: 'Let's go to Chios, Andronikos, to Chios. . . It's no distance from Vourla. . . Let's go, and if nothing happens we can always come back again. Your friend Kleomenes is going too, with his family. They're going in Andreas's caique. Please, Andronikos, please. . .' It was only then that you said: 'Let's go. . .' Only when I fell at your knees and wept. I know, I know you didn't believe me. You were just humouring me, like so many times before. And you made fun of me again when I took Persephone's ball, and made a hole and hid our valuables inside it.

Our Persephone was four years old in 1922. Do you remember, Andronikos. . .? Of course, how could you not remember. . .? She waved to you from the boat, and shouted:

'Daddy, hurry up. . .' And you were still arranging something with Kleomenes on the jetty when they arrived. . . First we heard the sound of running footsteps, then their shouting 'Get the Greeks. . . Get the Greeks!' and the night was all lit up by the torches the Turks were carrying. When your beautiful head fell in the sea, the water turned red. Our daughter screamed: 'Daddy, daddy!' And I threw myself into the sea. Why? Because I wanted to take you with me. You. Your beautiful head. The others hauled me up into the boat, and we rowed like madmen and managed to get to Andreas's caique. Other heads fell into the sea too. Kleomenes, and his boy, and Periklakis, Phroso's son. But it was yours that I wept for. Your beautiful head. I shall love you forever, Andronikos. You were the only man I ever loved. . . You know that. . . Only one thing I can't forgive you. . . Again and again I ask you, and you never answer. You tell me about other things, but never about this. I ask you again. Andronikos. Is our Persephone alive or dead. . .?

ELENI

'Mother. . . Mother. . . you're talking to yourself again. . .'

'I'm not talking to myself. I'm talking with Andronikos. Look – there, on the table, it's his head, can't you see. . .?'

'Yes, Mother, I see it. . .' (What am I supposed to say? She's going senile. She gets the past all mixed up with the present. In a minute she'll start telling me about Persephone again. . .)

'It hurts me, though, Eleni. Whenever I ask Andronikos about Persephone, he never answers. He must know. He's pure air, and goes where he will. He has the power to see the living and the dead. What do you think, Eleni? Is our Persephone still alive. . .?'

'She must be, Mother.'

It's always the same. She had so many children, but Persephone's the one she thinks about. Her first-born. People think that it's because she lost her... But Spyridoula died too. That was at the time when *it* first got hold of me. Mother's milk got infected because of the worry, and the baby died. We managed to baptize her in the air, calling her name three times... 'Spyridoula...' That's all the memorial she had. As for where our Yannis is buried, we have no idea. Some of the villagers took him away in '47. Our Yannis was twenty, then. We knew that they killed him, but where? Nobody knows. So mother has lost three children, but Persephone is the one she thinks about all the time. Maybe it's because the other two died, but Persephone disappeared from before her very eyes and she still can't bring herself to believe that she's dead, because there's just a chance that she isn't...

'Now that Dimitroula's here to look after you...'

'I don't need anyone to look after me. I can manage on my own, despite the fact that I can't see... Do I bother anyone...?'

'No, Mother, you're no trouble. And if it wasn't for you, I don't think I could have survived...'

'Don't talk like that. You're strong, you are. You're like me. The two of us and Fotos have kept this house going. So many children, so many mouths to feed, so many years... And now, after all that, here we are again, the three of us. Tell Dimitroula to keep an eye on Fotos, and you go and rest for a bit.'

'I think I'll go up for a while, up the hill. I think the Tree might speak to me tonight.'

'Let it get a bit darker first. Sometimes I think that the Tree has changed its ways too.'

I've washed myself all over, so as to be clean. I'm fasting. I've slept on the floor for several days. Today the Tree *must* speak to me. It must. I light incense, lie down by its roots, and wait. Nothing. I've come here six times since our Fotos fell ill. I ask the Tree: 'Will he get better? What can I do so that he doesn't have to suffer. . .?' Nothing. The leaves don't even move. But in the old days the Tree always had a message for us. However big or small the matter, it always had an answer.

I'm short of breath these days. I must be getting old. Forty-five years I've been coming here. Since I was eighteen. Together with my mother, who knew about these things. She used to listen to the leaves of the oak tree and she would understand. It was the woman with the metal sandals who taught her.

Mother told me about it. She said that night was coming on. She was searching for her Persephone. Day after day she searched. All day long she'd be walking, walking, never stopping. In the end her shoes wore out and dropped off her feet. She carried on walking, though, barefoot and hungry, like a mad woman. That night it was very damp, and Mother felt that her hair was wet, so she let it down to dry. All of a sudden, as she was standing there, she heard dogs barking. She was scared they might be wild dogs. The dogs came right up to her. Mother stood dead still, she said. Suddenly she saw a light, and a woman coming towards her, surrounded by dogs. 'A shepherdess,' thought Mother. 'But why does she have so many dogs?' And, so Mother says, her footsteps sounded strange on the ground. This puzzled her even more, so she looked down at the woman's feet. She wanted to see what sort of shoes she was wearing, to be making a noise like that. And then she saw her metal sandals. . .! Made of copper, they were. It was the first time Mother had seen anything like it. She'd never heard of people having shoes made of metal.

Then she looked up and saw the woman's face, and she froze
– the woman's eye sockets were empty...! Just empty, black
holes... So she was blind... That explained the dogs.

Then Mother said:

'I've lost my daughter.'

'I too have lost many things,' said the woman.

And the dogs howled more mournfully still, as if they
understood what was being said...

'I have come from far, far away,' said Mother, 'but I can't
find her anywhere.'

'I too am from far away, but also from nearby...'

'Where are you going at this time of night?' Mother asked,
feeling sorry for her.

'A woman is giving birth down below, in the village. I must
stand at her door,' the woman said. 'Can't you hear her
calling me?'

Mother says that, as hard as she tried, she couldn't hear a
thing. But the dogs were restless and wanting to move on.

'Let her wait, let her suffer a bit, like I had to suffer. And I
am not blind, as you think,' the woman said, as if reading
Mother's thoughts. 'I have eyes. It's just that I take them out.
So as to stay awake. Even so, I see everything.'

Mother was speechless. She was paralyzed with fear. What
kind of strange woman was this?

Before Mother could gather her wits, the old woman
continued: 'And you won't find your daughter in Kavala. Nor
in Philippi or Edessa. You have to go down, down to the
south. Listen carefully to the waters of the stream, and the
leaves of the lone oak tree. They will tell you where your
daughter is to be found. Everywhere you go, gather seeds and
keep them in your apron. Plant them when you finally set up
house. And if you find a pomegranate, take it with you.
Always take a pomegranate with you. And if you find your
daughter, give her some of it to eat. That way she will never
forget you. If you find her, that is...'

Mother ran after the woman, but she had already gone. A scream split the night. It was a woman screaming: 'Come quickly... That's enough... Don't make me suffer!'

MOTHER

My Eleni must be close now. She's getting older, and she moves more slowly these days. She gets out of breath going uphill. Now she'll be going up the little slope with the ancient stones. She'll let her hair down and she'll see the Tree in the distance. She'll lie at its roots, and embrace it and ask it to speak to her. To give her a message. Nothing will happen, though. I think the Tree has decided not to speak any more. I sense it. In the old days when I went, it used to tell me everything. I used to ask it about all sorts of things, big things and little things, and it would move its leaves and whisper its secrets to me. There was a stream nearby too. The stream used to murmur secrets of its own. I used to wash my body and my hair in the stream before I lay down to ask my questions. I felt it as if it was a man on top of me. A god-like man. A real oak it was, a huge tree. We were lovers. It always helped me. Later I took my Eleni to the Tree. I took her when her first blood came. 'She is yours,' I told it. 'You can love her as you have loved me, and now you can tell her your secrets too.' And so it turned out. From that moment the Tree used to speak to her too.

But it hasn't spoken to her for a year now. It won't speak to that granddaughter of mine either – Dimitra. She won't accept it. 'That's all rubbish,' she says. 'It's stupid. Trees don't talk.' I told the silly girl to stop it. But the Tree speaks to my Eleni less and less nowadays.

Fotos isn't going to last more than a fortnight. I can tell. We must write to Archontoula. She should come. She owes it to Fotos. She has to see him before he dies. And she must help with the garments. I'll tell my niece, Dimitroula, to write to her.

'Dimitroula. Take a sheet of paper and a pen from the drawer in the table and come here, because I need you.'

The wretched child didn't even want my name. 'What kind of name is that!' she said... I know that they call her Ritsa at home... Ritsa, I ask you...! Here she comes...

'Now, write what I'm going to tell you... Are you ready...?

> Dearly beloved daughter, greetings.
> We are in good health, and wish the same for you. My dear Archontoula, we have not written to you for many years, because we had no reason to trouble you. But now your beloved brother, Fotos, to whom we all owe so much, is not well. As soon as you receive this letter, come as fast as you can, so that you can see him while he is still alive. He wants to hear your voice before he dies. We are expecting you.
> Your mother, and your brothers and sisters.

'Did you write all that?'
'Yes.'
'Exactly as I said it?'
'Yes, of course...'
'Come here. Take this piece of paper. Tell me what it says... (Where is it? I always keep it at my breast... It must have slipped down... Ah there it is... It slipped under my petticoat.) There... Read what it says.'

'Mrs Archontoula Boura, 161 Sikinou, Kypseli, Athens.'

'That's the address of your aunt in Athens. Write it on this envelope, and give it to the postman when he comes this afternoon. Go on, and be quick about it, you hear. . .? So that Archontoula gets it in time. . .'

'What if Uncle Fotos gets up. . .?'

'I'm here. I shall sit next to him. And Eleni won't be long. . . She'll be back soon.'

Stupid child – she's left the door open again. The animals will get in. Oh well, let them come. . . Everything's passing. . . dying. . . And now my Fotos. . . Oh God, how many have I lost. . .! I have buried some of my children, and I have wept for others unburied. . . Andronikos. . . my Yannis. . . Spyridoula. . . Not my Persephone, though. I don't weep for her, because she's *alive*. . .! I know she is. . . I don't know where she is, but I *know* she's alive. . .

'Lie down, Fotos. Don't move around like that, you'll trip and fall. Do you want some water. . .? There, my first son, my sunshine, there, drink, don't be thirsty. . .'

'Mother. . .'

'Here I am, my warrior. . . What do you want. . .?'

He's fallen asleep again. But a strange sleep! It seems more like death. My Fotos must be at the gates of the Underworld by now. Down there with the flowers of the dead and their dogs. . .

'Eleni? Who's there. . .? Eleni. . .?'

'It's me, Mother, Eleni.'

'I knew it was. . . Why didn't you say something. . .? What's the matter, Eleni. . .? Did the Tree speak. . .?'

'Yes.'

'Tell me, then, tell me, what did it say? Tell me, don't torment me. . .'

'The Tree didn't say anything about us, Mother, or about Fotos. . . What it said had to do with itself. . . Like a riddle. . .'

'Tell me, child. . .'

'It said that palaces have fallen. And some "Apollo" has no house any more, nor a prophesying laurel. . . nor a talking spring. . . "The waters that once spoke," he said, "are now gone. . ." '

ROULA

I haven't seen my gay friend today. . . How's he going to get by without his yoghurt. . .? I'm telling you, that kid can't possibly *eat* all the yoghurt he buys. . . No way! He must be using it like face cream! A beauty mask! The other housewives in the neighbourhood aren't a patch on my gay friend. Every day you see him hanging out his socks, and sheets, and pillow cases, and his fancy pyjamas. . . Not to mention the dishcloths and the floorcloths. I don't even keep my towels as clean as he keeps his floorcloths! Yannis the butcher says that my friend buys steak by the kilo, but he doesn't eat it. . . He puts it on his face to keep his skin young. He's getting old, you see, and nowadays he's finding it harder to find boyfriends. . . But there you go, it's a free country – no reason why he shouldn't do what the hell he wants.

'Hi, Anna. Give us a pack of cigarettes – in case the army takes over again and we run out. . .'

I love the Savvaki girls. I've known them for ages. They grew up in the old man's shop. In those days they only had a little shop, but it was the centre of the neighbourhood. It had the only telephone, too. If you wanted to catch up with all the local gossip, you only needed to sit at your window, because

Yannis couldn't leave his shop and go ringing on doorbells, so he used to shout people's messages instead.

But then the neighbourhood started to grow. They built apartment blocks, Yannis's shop got bigger, and that was the end of it. We've been in Kypseli since 1946. In fact, my mother came here in 1943. To this part of town. At first we were living in a rented room in Limnou Street. I don't remember much about that. I was born in 1950.

Shit. . . . Where have my keys buried themselves. . .? Damn these handbags. . . Oh, there they are!

Looks like that's a letter sticking out of the old lady's mailbox. Can't be her pension, and it's a bit too early for bills. . . . Maybe somebody's remembered her. Let's have a look. We share a mailbox – that's why the name on the flap reads 'Boura-Veli'. Veli's the old lady. . . Here we go – one letter and a leaflet about a home typing course. Hang on a minute. . .! There's something weird here. . .!

'Mrs Archontoula Boura, 161 Sikinou, Kypseli, Athens.' I'd better put my things down for a minute. . . this is a bit creepy. Who could be writing to my mum. . .? My mum's been dead for years. . . What do you mean, 'Mrs Archontoula. . .'? Mrs Archontoula is pushing up daisies, for God's sake! Who can have sent it? What's it say on the back. . . 'Dimitra Chatsiphoti, Rizes Village, Larisa.'

Who the hell is Dimitra Chatsiphoti. . .? Hang on. . .! Chatsiphoti was my mother's maiden name before she married. . . It must be some relation of hers. . . Looks like someone's remembered us. . . What d'you reckon – maybe I've come into some money. I can tell them to stuff their job on the paper and join the landed gentry! Let's go upstairs and read it properly!

Stupid damn flat – can't see a thing unless you turn on the light!

'Dearly beloved daughter, greetings.'

(Ouf! Very old-fashioned! Wait a minute, though, it says 'daughter'! Dearly beloved *daughter*... So Dimitra Chatsiphoti must be my mum's mum! My grandma! I've got a grandma and I never even knew it...? Why didn't Mum ever tell me...? Anyway, what else does it say?)

'We are in good health, and we wish the same for you...'

(Bit wide of the mark there, old girl... Your daughter is in a far better place, as they say. You're a bit late with your letter, I'm afraid...)

'My dear Archontoula, we have not written to you for many years, because we had no reason to trouble you. But now your beloved brother Fotos...'

(That's the one...! Her brother Fotos! The only man in my mum's family that I know anything about. She was always going on about him. Fotos this and Fotos that... And his name was the last thing on her lips before she died.)

'...Your beloved brother, Fotos, to whom we all owe so much, is not well. As soon as you receive this letter, come as fast as you can to see him while he is still alive. He wants to hear your voice before he dies. We are expecting you. Your mother, and your brothers and sisters...'

So what do I do now? That's all I need, a village funeral...! Can't say I fancy the idea. I can't *not* go, though. No way... My mother did everything for me, all those years... Gave me all the love she had... took the bread out of her own mouth to feed me... So I promised her... before she died...

She'd been ill for days. No fever or pain, though. She said she was feeling a sort of weight in her chest. That's all. The doctor told me: 'Her heart is worn out. The hospital can't do anything for her. She needs complete rest.' Rest – you never met a more relaxed woman than my mum! God bless her. That afternoon I was worried about her, so I rang the doctor.

'She's coming to the end,' was all he said, and he gave me some drops to put in her water. Later on Mum started talking to herself, and shouting. 'Don't!' she said, and 'Fotos, save me, brother.' At about nine she came round again and said: 'If anyone ever tells you that my brother Fotos has died, I want you to promise me that you'll go for the funeral. I want you to kiss him, and throw a handful of earth onto his coffin before they cover him over. Promise me you'll do it. . .' I promised, and that seemed to calm her down. Her face became more relaxed. She fell into a peaceful sleep. Then at about twelve she had an attack. The ambulance men couldn't do anything for her. She died on the steps of the building. I had her buried in the Red Mill cemetery. The old lady next door came, and a couple of other neighbours and the girls from the office. And last year I did the re-burial.

I *have* to go. I promised, and that's that. The trouble is, where on earth is Rizes? I suppose it must be near Larisa. I'll try Antonis in the garage over the road. He's bound to have a map.

Now I see it! It's clear as day! My dream, I mean – now I see what it was about. . . It's obvious. Here we have a man, the column supporting the house – a family home which I didn't even know I had!

'Antonis, you're from Tithorea, so you ought to know. Where's Rizes?'

'Rizes – what do you mean, Rizes?'

'The village, idiot!'

'Let's try looking it up in the road atlas. Here, under R. . . Rivion Aitolo Akarnanias, Riviotisa Lakonias, Riza Aitolo Akarnanias, Riza Korinthias, Riza Prevezis, Riza Chalchidikis, Rizae Arkadias, Rozana Kilkis. . . It's not here!'

'That's impossible. . .!'

'Impossible or not, I'm telling you it's not here.'

'What am I supposed to do now? How will I get there?'

'Where's it near?'

'Larisa.'

'You'll just have to go to Larisa and ask from there.'

MOTHER

'Will my Archontoula remember the road? And the house? Will she remember to turn off at the crossroads and take the right path?'

He was bringing down animal skins. Stretched lambs' skins and young goats' skins. He was sitting up on the cart, on the wooden driving seat, and I was standing at the fork in the road, wearing my black clothes and holding my pomegranate. I'd done what the woman with the metal sandals had told me to do. I'd gone south, and I was asking everyone I met:

'Have you seen a little girl with a blue skirt and a little cross on her shoulder?'

I went through villages and hamlets and shepherds' pastures, and everyone I asked said no, so in the end all I said was:

'A girl. . . blue skirt. . . little cross on her shoulder. . .' And they all said 'No.'

And I was going further south all the time. By now I had reached the outskirts of Larisa. I saw a pomegranate sticking out through someone's fence. So I did what the woman with the metal sandals had told me. I stole the pomegranate.

I'd never seen such a pomegranate. It was huge. Come what may I would have taken it. Just as I was breaking it off, a girl came out of a gate in the fence. She looked me up and down. I must have looked like a gypsy. My clothes were hanging off me, and I had no shoes. The soles of my feet had become hard with walking barefoot. I used to dye them with henna, to make them red, because Andronikos liked that. And my hair was hanging down, unwashed and uncombed. . .

'Would you like a drink of wine, Auntie, to help you on your way. . .?'

'Auntie,' she called me. So that's what you've come to, Dimitra. . .! Once you were a goddess, and now you're 'auntie'. . . If Andronikos could have heard that! Twenty-three years old, and people were treating me like an old woman!

She took me into her cabin. She gave me some raki to drink, and some bean stew. 'Are you from round here?' she asked.

I shook my head, and immediately asked:

'A girl with a blue skirt and a little cross on her shoulder. Have you seen her?'

She didn't answer.

'Are you a refugee?' she asked. And before I could answer, she said: 'There are a lot of women who come looking for their lost sons and daughters here. Some looking for their husbands, too. . .' At that, we fell silent. What more could I say to her, or she to me. . .? Then she got up and went to a chest and pulled out some black clothes.

'Take these,' she said. 'They were my grandmother's before she died. They're quite clean – and she died of old age. Wear them. Don't walk around like that. . . I'm afraid I have no shoes to give you, though.'

I made the sign of the cross over her, and left. I had my pomegranate, and I had the black clothes. They were a complete outfit – a petticoat, a skirt, a blouse, a large head-scarf, and a knitted shawl. I went down to a deserted spot by the river, among the reeds. I took off my torn, dirty clothes and went and stood in the river. I washed and washed and I felt like a proper person again. I rinsed my hair again and again until I'd washed out all the dirt. I stood up to get dressed. And there, where the river waters hadn't been muddied, I saw the woman that Andronikos used to call his 'goddess'. The only difference was that I was thinner now, from being so tired and from walking so much. Andronikos's drawings on my body looked strange, considering the state of the rest of me. And it was then that I saw it, rolling down slowly on top of the water – Andronikos's beautiful head. That was the first time it appeared to me. I rushed to take hold of it. It never even occurred to me to wonder how Andronikos's head had got there, all the way from Vourla to a river in Larisa. I ran and tried to catch it, but it kept moving away. And I must have been making a noise as I splashed about in the water, shouting: 'Stop, Andronikos, stop and let me hold you. . .' And the women who were doing their washing further down must have heard my shouting, and they came to look. And when they saw me they froze. And I froze too. I was naked, with Andronikos's drawings on my body, from my breasts down. . . What must they have thought?

One of the women started screaming: 'Run, run. . . Don't you see, she's a witch. . . She'll steal our voices. . .'

And before I could make a move to say, 'No, I'm not a witch,' they had all run off in terror.

I dressed as quickly as I could and hid my own clothes under a rock. The only thing I kept was my white petticoat. Or, rather, it *was* white once, with lace and embroidery. But it was now full of holes and grey with dirt, and all patched, with the little pockets where I kept my seeds. All kinds of seeds. Sorrel, spinach, lentils, basil, marjoram, beetroot, cauliflower, buck-beans, limes, peas, yellow marigolds, and all different colours of carnations. I'd had a mania for seeds. Some I picked and some I found. I stitched them into little pouches which I sewed into my petticoat. I thought, 'When I find my Persephone, I shall make a little garden the like of which has never been seen in all the world. But first I must find her.'

When I was dressed, I wrapped my headscarf round tightly to hide my blonde hair. My hair was golden-yellow again now that I had washed it. Better for me to look like an old 'auntie' than a twenty-three-year-old. I had seen and heard many things. . .

I went on for a bit and came to a crossroads. I had no idea where I was or where I was going. I only knew the reason. 'I have to find my daughter,' I told myself. 'I have to find my daughter.'

It was then that I saw the man on the cart. But I ignored him until he stopped and asked me:

'Are you going that way, lady?'

I bowed my head. I didn't want him seeing how young I was. . . He took this to mean no, and on he went.

I was tired. Very tired. I'd been heading further and further south, and I still hadn't found my daughter. What was I to do . . .? What would become of me. . .? Winter was coming. . . I stood there at the crossroads like an idiot. The road that the cart-driver had gone down was narrow and winding. The other road was wider, and looked as if it went to Larisa. And who knew where the third road went. . .? And anyway, what did I care. . .? I stood there as though in a trance. . . At first I thought I was seeing things again. But now I am sure: it was a marble column. Right at the crossroads. Why hadn't I noticed it before? It was a square column. I went over to look. It had a carved head on it, carved all round like a proper head. I recognized that head, even though it was carved out of marble. That's why I went over. It was the beautiful head of my Andronikos. . . and. . . Lord. . .! What else did I see. . .? The sign of his manhood – his testicles – carved on each side of the column. . .

'Andronikos – why all this...? This is the second time you've shown yourself to me today... The first time, in the river, as I knew you from before, floating in blood... And now your head, carved four times into a marble column...? And your testicles...? What is all this...? Why don't you speak, my angel...? Say something, show me... Give me a sign... Andronikos... Andronikos... There's no life in your eyes... but you're trying to tell me something... What are you trying to say...?'

I stroked Andronikos's beautiful head, I spoke to him as though he was still alive, I kissed his lips... They were cold, dead, yet they responded to my kiss, I'm sure of it... And I stroked his testicles, without feeling shame... 'Andronikos... Andronikos...'

I didn't even hear the cart come up behind me. It stopped right next to me while I was talking to Andronikos. It was just as well that I wasn't still stroking him and kissing him.

'Are you going up the hill, lady...?' the driver asked.

I didn't answer. I clutched the pomegranate tight and watched my Andronikos. His eyes were looking far, far away, not at me any more. The driver went 'Whooah' and held his horses. He seemed to be sorry for me... because I'd been standing there for hours... and because he had taken me for an old woman. He got down from his cart and came over to me. On one side of me I had Andronikos's marble column, and on the other side, this man.

'Are you going up?' he asked again.

I shook my head, to say 'No', and then he realized. I sensed that he had realized. He rolled his eyes and looked at me, and looked again... I felt his eyes ranging over my face... I too had become a marble column... He pulled at my headscarf and my hair fell down my back. It reached as far as my waist...

I had rubbed the hair that showed outside the scarf with ash, so that it looked grey... but the rest was blond...

'What eyes... What eyes... What hair!' You could hardly hear his voice. His lips were barely moving. Just a whisper...

I was scared. I was scared of him. I could smell sex on him. He smelt as if he'd been with a woman. He smelt of patchouli. ... He was sated with woman... for the moment...

'Where are you going?' he asked.

I shrugged my shoulders. Where was I going? How should I know. I was going south, south... but where to, I didn't know. Something about him frightened me. And I frightened him too. I don't know why, but I sensed it. Maybe it was because he had thought I was an old woman, and then discovered I was young... Or maybe it was something else...

'Where have you come from?' he asked.

I shrugged my shoulders again. What could I tell him? The story of my life...? And anyway, why should I...? He was a stranger... In a little while he'd be gone... Next to me was Andronikos, silent, staring into the distance.

The man stood there, not knowing what to do. He needed to get a move on, because it was getting dark, but at the same time he couldn't tear himself away... Suddenly he took my hand and looked at my palm. It was a hand that had seen a lot of work... With tobacco, cotton, sheep – wherever I happened to be. The main thing was that I was on the road south... I'd had no problems with men. I used to hide my face and wrap myself up in my headscarf with only my nose showing... Only one time, when I was looking for work, did a man try to touch me, but I went to scratch his eyes out... Needless to say, I lost the job...

'If you want a job, we have work. Not in the fields. In the house. My mother is a widow. And my grandmother, Maria, has gone senile. My mother is fed up with going to the house to look after her. The old lady wanted to stay in her own house. We don't have anyone who can help her out. If you want. . .'

As he was saying all this he seemed to be in a hurry. Was he in a hurry for me to accept. . .? Or in a hurry to be on his way. . .? I turned to Andronikos. He had vanished. . . I didn't know what was going on. . . I had kissed him, and stroked him, and felt the marble with my hands and my lips. . . What was happening. . .? Was I starting to go mad. . .? Was I seeing ghosts. . .?

'Come on,' he said. 'It's getting dark. You'll see. You'll get on well with the old lady. She tells stories, dozens of stories. You'll enjoy listening to them.' He took me by the hand. He led me to the cart and helped me up. I did all this as if I was sleep-walking. I was thinking of Andronikos and how he was always so loving to me. . . The man helped me up next to him on the wooden seat of the cart. He gave me the headscarf. 'Wear it properly, because we're going through the village now,' he said.

I gathered up my hair as best I could and wrapped my scarf across my mouth and tied it behind my head so that my cheeks and forehead were covered. Suddenly the headscarf had become a kind of protection. As if it was looking after me. As if it had a power to ward off evil.

A mist had come down all around. It was autumn and the leaves on the trees were all turning red and yellow. They looked magical in the mist and twilight. There was a big forest on both sides of the road. Chestnut and hazel trees, planes and poplars. And there was water running everywhere. Little rushing streams, and little waterfalls falling down the rocks. And the mist was getting ever thicker.

The man took an umbrella, opened it, and gave it to me. I had my pomegranate in one hand and the umbrella in the other.

'We're almost there,' he said.

Almost where...? There was not a house in sight... No sound of dogs barking... We took a side-turning, and the road started going uphill. In the distance a small bell-tower came into sight. We came closer. The bell-tower had a clock too, but it had no hands. What time could it have been...? Or what day, come to that...? I wasn't even sure what month it was. Late October? Early November...?

ROULA

God – that man sitting next to the priest is the spitting image of Sotiris. Could be his double. I actually thought it was him, for a moment. But then I thought, what would Sotiris be doing on a long-distance bus to Larisa...? He'd have gone in his Mercedes, with its air conditioning and smoked glass windows and you wouldn't have seen him for dust...

The old lady next to me is starting to get on my nerves. She's on her way to see her daughter, who's had a baby, so she's going to help out... So who the hell cares?! Some women these days seem to have a mania for children. To hell with them. Nothing but trouble. My mother knew all about that – she had a hard time with me. Not to mention when the kids are sick. Sotiris was right, you know. When I got pregnant, I wanted to keep it to start with. It was my first time, you see. But Sotiris got it all sorted out for me, no problem. He had a friend who was a doctor, and he made an appointment for me the very next morning.

That Sotiris was a proper little mafioso. I was sixteen at the time, and I was working in the dark room. Well, not actually *in* the darkroom. I had a desk outside, with a lightbox on it, and I had to spot out any little holes in the negatives, with a special fluid and a paint brush. I used to get bored spotting out holes all day, but the wages were pretty decent. And I could chat with the others, so the days went by quite fast, really.

The fluid looked like melted chocolate, and we had to close the lid tight when we went home because cockroaches are crazy for the stuff. It's a special treat for cockroaches. I remember one time I deliberately left the lid off to see what would happen, and the next day you could see the marks where the roaches had been nibbling it...

Anyway, one afternoon I ran into Sotiris as I was leaving work. Up till then I'd always called him 'Mr Sotiris'. He said: 'Since it's raining, and since we live near each other, why don't I run you home?' I jumped at the chance, because there weren't a lot of Mercedes around in those days, and I'd certainly never been in one. What really got me were the buttons that made the windows go up and down... I mean – imagine what it must have cost! Like they say, if you've got it, flaunt it! Anyway, when he invited me to come into the house while he sorted out a few papers, I never gave it a second thought. I was dying to see what the place looked like from the inside.

God, the luxury...! It was carpeted right through with a beige carpet. A round pink divan in one corner. One of those table lamps with bubbles in it, that makes all different patterns. He showed me the house, and he was really proud of it. I could see tell that. And, to be honest, who wouldn't have been? And what about the bed...! The sort of bed you only see in films... Shaped like a clam shell, with concealed lighting and a soft mattress. He told me to try it, to see how soft it was... I saw for myself how soft it was, and the rest goes without saying... Then he said something that really bugged me. He asked me if I was clean...

'I take a shower every day,' I said.

'That's not what I mean,' he said. 'You haven't got VD or something?'

Anyway, I ended up learning a thing or two, about sex, about VD, and just about everything else. And I also ended up pregnant, and when I told him he said: 'Don't worry. I've got a friend who's a doctor. He'll get you sorted out straight away. And don't worry about the money, I'll see to it.'

'I hadn't expected that kind of behaviour from Sotiris, mug that I was. I was only sixteen, so what did I know about life? I thought that when a man got you pregnant, he married you. . . I found out the hard way.

Anyway, the next day I set off to see his friendly doctor. He had a clinic in Vathis Square. That morning everything seemed to go wrong. It was like a nightmare. . . I told my mum that I had to do some work out of town, so she wouldn't try ringing me during the day. I managed to get a cab. It went about fifty yards, then ground to a halt. The driver said it was the clutch. I wanted to tell him where he could stick his clutch. . . My appointment was for eight, and it was already twenty to, and I was still right near my house. So I rushed around and found another cab. There were two women inside, going to Stadiou Street, and the cabby was idling along like he had all the time in the world. 'Any chance you could go a bit faster,' I said. 'I'm in a hurry.' 'If you're in a hurry, why don't you walk?' he said. The women were giving me dirty looks. I wondered whether they suspected something, but then I thought I was being paranoid. In the end I got out at Veranger and decided to walk to Vathis Square. I thought about calling the whole thing off – not going through with it. . . And in eight months I'd have a baby. . .

I got to the clinic. The doctor was there, but he was seeing someone else. I sat on a bench and waited. There were other girls waiting too. A couple of them must have been with their husbands, because they had wedding rings. The rest were like me . . . on their own. The doors would open, and a woman would come out, white as a sheet . . . I wanted to be sick . . . I was scared . . . 'I'm going,' I thought, but I didn't. I stayed. There were four doctors on duty. One girl was crying her eyes out when she came out. 'Bastards,' I thought. 'The men have all the fun, and we pay the price. It's not fair. Men and women should take it in turns – we have one, and then *they* have one. Not just babies. Abortions as well. . .'

The doctor called me. 'Roula,' he said, like he was saying 'Next please!' and then he waited to see which one of us was Roula. He took me into an office. He asked me if my pregnancy test had been positive, and I said yes. Then he told me to get my top half undressed so that he could look at my breasts. Like an idiot, I thought that was what you had to do. . . . So that fucking doctor – I hope he dies and his balls drop off – started sucking my tits. First one, and then the other. And what the bloody hell was I supposed to do. . .? Run away? But where to? If I ran off, who'd do the abortion. . .? Because now I really *wanted* it done. . . I *wanted* it. . . I wanted to get rid of every shred of Sotiris that was inside me, and I never wanted to lay eyes on him again. . .

When the doctor finished groping me, he told me to get dressed and come into the surgery.

There were three other girls getting ready. I took off my shoes, my tights and my skirt, which just left my blouse, bra and knickers on. . . They pointed to the operating table. It was one of those where you have to lift your legs up and open them. . . I got up and put my feet in the holder. Then the anaesthetist came in, and Sotiris's friendly doctor.

'You were quick enough getting them off last time,' the doctor said, 'so how come you're so slow this time?' He was right. I'd forgotten to take my knickers off. . . I was so scared that they'd start the operation before I was properly asleep. . .

So I swallowed this insult along with the rest, took my knickers off and climbed up again. . .

'Please, don't start before I'm properly asleep. . .' I whispered.

I felt like a four-year-old. I said to myself: 'I'll get this over with and I never want to see another man again. . .'

The doctor sat down facing my open legs. He took an instrument from a table with a lot of things on it and pushed it into me.

'Don't start before I'm asleep,' I shouted.

The other one who'd strapped my legs to the table said, 'Relax, girl.' He put an elastic strap round my arm and gave me a jab with a hypodermic. Just before I passed out I saw the doctor pushing another instrument into me, with knobs on the end of it.

When I woke up, I was in a bed. A terrible way to wake up. There was another girl in the bed next to me. My hands and feet felt freezing. The girl next to me was crying, sobbing in her sleep. . . I dozed off again, and then woke up properly.

A nurse came in and gave us a prescription for some antibiotics.

I went out. I had to go out through the waiting room. There were more women waiting there. Horrible, filthy fucking place! Bastards! All these women, led off to the slaughter. . .

I rang Sotiris. 'OK,' I said, 'it's over. Only I have to lie down and take it easy today, and I can't go home.' He told me to go to his place, and he said he'd come too.

He came, let me in, and then rushed off. I lay down on the settee. I loathed his sea-shell bed. And I loathed Sotiris. And men. . . All of them. . .

I gave him a hard time of it in the office for the next few days. I went round calling him by his first name. I was saying things like: 'I don't think I'll be up to it today, Soti...' I almost lost him his job. A proper little scandal... And me being under-age... But what did I understand about all that...! Anyway, he sent me up to work in the office, just to get rid of me... Jesus, it makes me angry just to think about it... And I thought I'd forgotten all about it. It's amazing – some little thing reminds you, and all of a sudden, whoosh, you're right back there. Cool it, Roula... let's light up... The old lady next door's started up with the same old story: 'Cancer... cigarettes give you cancer...' I was about to tell her to get lost, but I stopped myself.

ELENI

I'll put Archontoula in the middle room with Mother. They'll have so much to talk about. And anyway I have to look after Fotos. Somebody has to keep an eye on things. We have to prepare a proper reception for our sister. It's been so many years...

'How many years has Archontoula been gone, Eleni?'

(There she goes again – how on earth does the woman manage to get into your head like that...? Can she read our minds, or what...? That's why she scares everyone... I don't know how she does it. I couldn't...)

'It must be forty years, now, Mother.'

'Forty-one years this year. It was '43, wasn't it...?'

'You're right. Since I'm fifty-eight now, and Archontoula is two years younger than me, she must have been eighteen when she went...'

'She's not two years younger than you. She was born in '25. Bring me the St Nicholas icon so that we can see. I've got the names of all the children written on the back, and the years they were born.'

'I'm sure you're right, Mother, if you say so.'

'Bring me the icon, anyway.'

(What on earth does she want the icon for? She knows it off by heart. And the pencil on the wood is so faint that you can barely read it anyway...)

'Now, you see, there... read it. Doesn't it say: Fotos and Eleni, 1924; Archontoula 1925; Thodoroula 1926; Yannis (God rest him) 1927; Tassos 1929; Spyridoula (may the Lord rest her soul...) 1931; Despo 1933?'

'It does, Mother. You're right. Someone must keep an eye out for Archontoula. It's so many years since... Maybe she won't remember the way...'

'Of course she'll remember, bless her... Of course...How could she not remember...?'

'I'm going to feed the chickens. It's getting late.'

MOTHER

It's getting dark. I don't see the evening coming, any more. I hear it, though. There's a cockerel, must be a very small one. It crows at four in the morning, at dawn, and then at about six in the evening, when it's starting to get dark.

It was getting dark when we arrived outside the village. What sort of woman would the old lady turn out to be? A strange old lady, for sure, for her daughter-in-law not to want her in the house...

He slowed down in front of a big two-storey house, and said: 'This is where my mother lives, and my brothers and sisters, and me...'

The house was well-built, like the others in the village, with dressed stone, a verandah, and arched lintels over the doors and windows. I couldn't see it very well in the dusk. We left the village behind and took a winding road up a hill. At the top you could see a little white chapel. It was only when we got closer that I saw that it wasn't a chapel. It was a house. An unusual sort of house. Completely white, with little windows like a monastery and a wooden door. And next to the door was an anchor. . .! As high as the door, and with a chain that was as thick as a man's ankle. What on earth was an anchor doing in the middle of the plain of Thessaly. . .? Who had brought it there. . .? And where from. . .? What was this new mystery. . .? And the whole place was silent as the grave. Not a sound – no animals, no dogs, nothing. Just the sound of a screech-owl. I took it as an omen.

He pushed open the door and we went in. As I looked at the house it reminded me of the houses back home: they had internal courtyards too. Protected from the eyes of the Turks. And there used to be stone benches that ran around the walls outside, and sweet-smelling flowers. There was a stone retaining-wall here too, but from what I could see in the dark the plants were all dead and withered. There was a light coming out of a room facing us. We went towards it. 'Don't worry if the old lady starts saying strange things. She's almost a hundred and twenty years old. She's had enough of life. . .!'

He opened the door and we went in. An old woman was sitting at a table. An old, old woman. All skin and bone. She had a lighted lamp, with the wick turned down so low that you could hardly see a thing.

'Is that you, Demos?' the old woman asked.

'Who else could it be? I've brought a woman to look after you. Don't make things difficult for her. I'm going, because it's dark. I'll come back tomorrow.'

He went, and shut the door behind him. Then I heard the

outside door shut and the cart pull away. The old woman had this strange way of shaking her head all the time. She would look at the wall and then start shaking her head again.

She turned back and said, 'He's late.'

Who was late. . .? I thought that the old woman lived all alone. . .

'He's late. And I told him to be here before it got dark. How can I cope on my own with five children. . . And where did I put the gruel? I can't find it anywhere. . .'

I stood and watched her. 'The old lady must be senile,' I thought. 'Especially since he said she's a hundred and twenty. Anyway, that can't be true. . . Do people live that long? Of course they don't! He must have been lying.' Then the old woman said: 'Sit down. Come and sit by me. I can't see any more. My eyesight's gone. What's your name? Where are you from? Are you Demos's mistress?'

I jumped as if I'd been bitten by a snake. 'I'll leave if you're going to talk to me like that,' I said, emphatically. 'He said that there was work for me, and that's why I'm here.'

'All right, all right. Don't go. I need someone to talk to. They keep me here all on my own. I can't bear the loneliness. Don't go, eh. . .? Don't go. . . I'll give you. . . what can I give you, since they've taken everything from me? You won't go, will you, eh? All right. . . Shall we make some sage tea to cheer ourselves up? Look, you'll find the sage over there in the little box next to the stove. There's water in the kettle. . .'

Kuyum, she said, for kettle. And *alisfakiya*, for sage. Those are *our* words. From Asia Minor. They don't use them here – they say *mastrapa* and *faskomilia*. . .

'Where do you come from,' I whispered. I don't know why, but I was scared of what she would answer.

'From Psara, my child,' the old woman said, and there was pride in her voice.

'And I'm from Asia Minor too, from Vourla,' I said.

'I was sixteen years old in 1824. I'd already had my Thodoros and my Aretoula. I was pregnant with Pelagia. My husband, a captain, was fighting the Turks. . .

'We weren't at war with them. We lived among them, and everything was fine. They didn't bother us and we didn't bother them. But when the Greek army went and took Smyrna. . . we took out the Greek flags that we had in our trunks, and put them out on our balconies. . .

'My captain was Kanaris's righthand man. He was with him when he went to Pontos and Odessa. And he was with him when they burned Kara Ali's flagship. And he was with him again in Samos, when they burned Hosref's frigate.'

'My husband, Andronikos, had a tannery at Dere, near the Great Bridge. He used to draw, too. Saints, and icons, and Alexander the Great. Just for the fun of it. And one day he marked a little cross on the shoulder of my daughter, Persephone.'

'On the twenty-fourth of June, eighteen twenty-four, the saint's day of Saint Zacharias and Saint Elizabeth, and the birthday of John the Baptist, the Turks began bombarding Psara. We fought and fought, but in vain. The Turks came ashore in their boats. And then the terror began. Women were throwing themselves into the sea with their babies, to escape. They locked some of our people into the Old Fort and blew them up. My husband put us aboard a caique – me, still pregnant with my Pelagia, and with my two little ones, one of them still at my breast. . . We made for the open sea. . .'

'My Andronikos made fun of me. He didn't believe that the Turks would kill us. It was only when I fell at his feet that he finally agreed to go. Only because I fell at his feet, though, not because he believed me. We were going to escape to Chios, on Andreas's caique. Chios is almost no distance at all from Vourla. . . My Persephone was four, then . . . The child and I got into the rowing boat, and then the caique.

Andronikos was on the jetty sorting something out with Kleomenes and his boy... Andronikos's head was the first to fall in the water... Andronikos's beautiful head made the sea all red... Then other heads fell. Kleomenes... and his boy... The Turks cut the heads off any man they caught... But I was only concerned for my Andronikos...'

'Other caiques were heading for Monovasia. My husband was angry. He said that we should fight them at sea, with our boats, but the others wouldn't listen to him. They said they should fight on dry land. They wouldn't even listen to Kanaris, and so the disaster happened. My husband steered his caique towards the opposite shore, to the coast over by Pilion.'

The old woman stopped talking, just like a match that flares up when you light it, and then goes out... that was how she was... Talk, talk, talk, all in one go, and then silence. Her mind was far off in foreign parts. With her captain and her children. I fell silent too... lost in my own thoughts. My mind was all over the place. I was thinking of my daughter, my Persephone. Wondering where she was... Hoping that she was with good, compassionate people, and that nothing bad had happened to her....

'Lie down next to the hearth and sleep,' the old woman said. 'But don't put the lamp out.'

I spread two rugs on the floor and lay down. I couldn't close my eyes, though... The old woman was sitting at the table, and you couldn't tell whether she was asleep or awake. Later on I realized that she never really slept.

As I settled down, she started rambling again, talking to her captain. She was complaining, telling him it was time to stop somewhere. It seemed like he wasn't taking any notice. Then she started writhing round in her chair and groaning. I was worried for her, and got up out of bed. She was shouting that she was about to give birth, and that he would have to stop the cart. 'Yanni,' she shouted, 'my captain, stop. Stop – can't you see? The baby's coming. Stop under a plane tree somewhere. My time has come.'

I washed her forehead with water from the kettle and stroked back a few loose strands of hair.

'Relax, love,' I told her, 'Relax. It's a dream. Look, can't you see? You're in your own room. With me.'

I'd forgotten that the old lady was blind and couldn't see. When she got over the upset, she asked me something strange. She wanted me to give her my hand. She took it and stroked it and felt it all over and put it next to her cheek. She held it there for an hour, and I just had to stand there. I couldn't even budge. My palm was all wet.

The old woman was sobbing silently. The fact that she was crying without making any noise made me feel very strange. Maybe if she'd been crying properly I wouldn't have given it a second thought. But here she was, a little old lady, no bigger than a child, crying without a sound.

'Come on, grandma,' I said. 'It's over now.' And then the wailing started. A low, groaning moan.

'Don't do that, love,' I said. 'Come on. . .'

When she finally got over it, she told me. At the start she had been crying about all the unhappy things in her life, and then she'd been crying because I had called her grandma. Nobody had ever called her grandma before. It was always 'old woman this' and 'old woman that'. To call someone grandma shows love, she said. 'Old woman' shows disrespect, a lack of caring. . .

I thought about what the old granny had said, and now that I'm a grandmother too I know what she meant. . .

I begged her to lie down, so that we could go to sleep. But no, she insisted on staying there in her chair.

'You see,' she said, 'for me day and night are the same. Darkness. If I lie down in bed, I worry that the Archangel will come to take me. Not that I'm scared of him – I'm just not ready yet. I feel better here, in my chair. When the dawn comes, though, I shall go and have a little lie down.'

She couldn't see the dawn when it came, but she could hear it. And the cockerels and the other birds, and the noises of the other animals waking up. . . Then she went over to her little divan and lay down and fell into a sort of half-sleep. . .

ELENI

What's Mother doing now. . .? Is she sleeping. . .? It's weird, this habit she has of not lying down to sleep at night. . . She never lets me relax. . . Always getting up and poking around. . . It's dark now. It's getting dark early these days. . . If Fotos wasn't so ill, I would carry on making the rug I've got on the loom. Even the sound of footsteps wakes him, though, and he starts shouting again. . . I must do something. I can't just sit here doing nothing. . . I'll go crazy. . . Maybe I could cut those rags up, to make a mat for the floor. But then again, it would be bad luck to use the scissors while Fotos is like this. . . I can't do anything. . . So maybe I'll just sit.

If I lose Fotos and Mother. . . I won't have anyone left to talk to. . . My brothers and sisters have left. . .I'll have nobody but the chickens, the cat and the pigeons to talk to. . . And what about this creepy house. . . I'll go away. . . I'll pack my things and leave. . . Maybe I could go into a convent. . . No, I couldn't. . . That would be just wasting my life. . . It's not for me. And anyway I have other things in my life. . . the things I'm used to. . . the Tree. . . Ouf. . . I'll just stay here and this can be my convent. With my own rules and my own prayers. . .

'Try to relax, Fotos. . . Don't, you'll tire yourself out. . .! Do you want a bit of water. . .? No. . .? What then. . .? She's coming, my love, she's coming. . . Our Archontoula is on her way. . . Look, I'll mop your forehead with vinegar water, to cool you. . . Don't, Fotos. . . Stop it, you've knocked it over. . .! Don't torment me, brother. . .!

'His torment is far worse than yours, my daughter. . .! His is the true torment, the last torment. . .!'

Mother is right. As always, she is right. . .

'It's going to rain. . . Have you brought the washing in, Eleni?'

'Yes. But I don't think it'll rain. . . There's not a cloud in the sky. You can see all the stars, Mother.'

'Hmm. . . There's a smell of rain on the breeze. . . And the window on the south side is banging. . . Latch the windows properly, in case the banging wakes Fotos. . . And make sure all the animals are in.'

MOTHER

I knew a storm was on its way. I could feel it in my hair. I went like this with my hand, and my hair was all prickly. My skirt was blowing up at the knee. The whole place was groaning. . . So much wind and rain all at the same time. . . Rain is good for the crops – but wind . . .

When it used to blow like this in Vourla, my late aunt would light the Resurrection candle next to her oil lamp. She would kneel and you would see her lips moving. . . My uncle Theotokis had a caique, you see..

The wind has dropped a bit, but the rain is still falling in torrents. . . The bell. . .! Yes, yes, I'm sure of it. . . It's the bell. . .

'Eleni. . .! It's the bell! The Saint has returned. . .'

'I heard him, Mother. When the sun comes up I'll go and clear up.'

'I shall come too. We'll go up gently. . . It's been a long time since I last went, and who knows if I can still make it. . .'

It was years ago that I first heard the bell. When I had just arrived here. I remember it was raining, and the wind was blowing hard. . . It had been pouring all afternoon. . . It was evening, and I was giving grandma her soup. The two of us were getting on well. Very well, in fact. I would wash her, because they hadn't bathed the poor woman in years, and I would delouse her. It was unbelievable, the number of lice on her head. . . I put a bowl of boiling water between her legs, and I combed the lice out and into the water, and they went pfft and burst. Then I would rinse her hair with vinegar, and in the morning when the sun came up I would pull out the lice eggs one by one. I squashed them between my fingernails. Some of them were empty and some not. Slowly I won grandma's confidence. And she opened her heart to me. Both of us loved our poor departed husbands. We used to talk about them all the time. We didn't talk a lot about children, though. I didn't want to talk about Persephone. She understood and kept off the subject.

That evening the wind and rain were making such a noise that we didn't get a wink of sleep. I sat next to her by the lighted lamp, and got on with some knitting. Grandma, as was her habit, was rocking her head to and fro. It was a while since I had last seen Andronikos, either awake or in my dreams. In fact I hadn't seen him since that time at the crossroads. I wondered whether he was angry that I was spending the winter here instead of heading south to look for my daughter. I asked grandma if she ever saw her late husband in her dreams. 'No,' she said, 'I don't see him. But I hear him all the time. And not when I am asleep, but when I'm awake. He thought of everything, you know, and this too – that I should hear his voice even though he's dead.'

I didn't understand what she meant, but I didn't say anything. After an hour like this, without my saying anything – this was grandma's habit – she began to tell me a story. Her late husband, she said, had hated the sea so much that when he traded in his caique for the cart, he decided to keep one of the oars. Grandma didn't know why her captain had kept his oar. What was the use of one oar? But he had a plan. Wherever they arrived, he would show people the oar, and he would ask: 'Look at this, friend. Do you know what it is?' And the reply would come: 'It's an oar, of course.' And the captain would whip up the animals and set off again. 'I shall build my house and settle my roots in a place where people have never seen the sea, never seen a caique, never seen boats and never seen oars. When I show them my oar, and they tell me that it's a lump of wood, and not an oar, that's where I'll stop and settle!'

So it was that they ended up in Rizes. Here, when he showed them the oar they said that it was just a piece of wood. 'But the sea is like a canker,' grandma said. 'Once you have seen it you can never forget it. When my captain decided to settle here and built the house, everyone was amazed. They'd never seen a house like that before. He had told the builders to build him a fisherman's house. What did they know about arched doors and windows...? And courtyards and cisterns...? Ha! And one day, a bit later, I saw some gypsies coming up... They had a cart, with something in iron on it... They stopped outside our door and began unloading it... It was an anchor...! Yes, really...! The only thing my captain was upset about was that they hadn't finished off the edges as they should have done... Oh well...'

Again I didn't understand. I was still waiting for her to tell me how she heard her captain in her sleep, but she had gone off onto another story. I lay down on the little sofa and fell asleep. I was woken by the old lady shaking me.

'Do you hear it?' she asked.

I heard a bell ringing in the dark, and the sound of the rain falling endlessly.

'Do you hear?' she said again. 'St Nicholas is on his travels. Today he went to calm the waters. Now he's come back. He's shaken the seaweed off him, and he's filled his little chapel with seaweed. He always comes back just after midnight. Then he rings his bell, which means: come and clean my chapel. So you must go, early tomorrow morning, to clean it. My captain built the chapel. It's identical with the chapel of St Nicholas in Psara.'

And, just as she always did, she fell silent again. She would tell the story she had to tell all in a rush. . . and then she would be silent. Was she thinking. . .? Or trying to remember something. . .? Impossible to know. . .!

The bell carried on ringing all night. I thought it might have been the wind, but the wind had stopped blowing. Not that I had believed grandma's story. I told myself that she must be confused. I closed my eyes, but the bell wouldn't let me sleep. It wasn't a festive or a mourning sort of ringing. It had a different sort of rhythm. Dong, then it stopped for a moment, then ding-ding-ding, then it stopped for another moment, and then off it went again... Was somebody ringing it in the night... in the rain? Strange...! Surely the wind couldn't ring a bell rhythmically like that, with those regular pauses... Of course it couldn't.... But over these last two years I'm no longer sure of anything.... Everything that was ever solid in my life has turned to dust and scattered. And everything that was unsure and uncertain has become like stone, standing there... Everything's gone – my Andronikos, my daughter, my house, my village, Asia Minor... I have nothing left...

At daybreak grandma shook me. 'Come here,' she said, 'and I shall tell you about our little church. As you come out of the garden and turn right, you go up a slope. You will pass some large stones. People say they are ancient stones. Go on up the hill; you will pass the Tree, and you will see the chapel on a hill. There is a broom behind the cypress tree. Sweep up the seaweed and put it in a little pile outside the church. When it dries, you will go up and burn it.'

'Grandma's strange ideas,' I thought, and I got up. I had been with her for ten days now. She never let me go out. She was scared that I would disappear and she would be left on her own. A couple of times a little boy came – her grandson, or great-grandson, who knows? – and brought us a little meat and cheese. Apart from that not a soul set foot in her house. I wanted to go out. I was longing to go for a walk, for the freedom that walking gives you. As I went out I heard her calling after me: 'Don't be late coming back, eh. . .'

Grandma had a large garden. At the other end of the garden she had a shed, a long wooden shed, which was roofed with planks. We had that sort of thing in Vourla too. But her garden had gone to ruin. Some sorrel was growing, and dandelions and thistles. Nothing else. And there I was with a petticoat full of all kinds of seeds. . . But I hadn't saved them for other people's gardens. . . I would only plant them when I found my daughter, Persephone. . . For the moment I let them travel around with me, in my petticoat. . . I found the rising ground on the right, and took it. Stony and barren, it was. Donkey thistles, dried out by the summer. Like the countryside round Vourla. . . And there were the ancient stones that grandma had spoken of. Fine stones. Round, they were, like little mill-stones, except that they had two ledges running round them, like seats. What on earth were seats doing on a threshing floor. . .? Strange. The stones were still wet from the rain the day before, but I sat down anyway, to take a rest, because I had done the climb all in one go.

I sat on the bottom step, and leaned back against the step above. It was so quiet and peaceful. . .! I felt so relaxed. I was stroking the shiny stone in my right hand, just like this, and I could feel it had lines on it. I turned it over, and saw that there were letters carved into the stone. Ancient letters. Andronikos had told me about the ancient letters. Oh, Andronikos. . . If only you were here . . .! You could have read the message that your ancients carved. But there I was – I looked and I looked, but the letters weren't at all like the letters I'd learned in my little bit of schooling. Hmm. . . Maybe this second letter is a capital L, I thought. An ancient Greek L, that is. The ancients used to do their letters in this sloping sort of way. Oh well. I should go, in case I'm late and grandma starts to worry. And here's the tree. It's a handsome tree! And there's a little spring nearby. . . On my way back I'll stop and rest, and have a wash. I feel ashamed to wash at grandma's.

The chapel had a bell without a rope, and a little parapet running round it. I found the broom behind the cypress tree. 'Right,' I thought, 'let's sweep the chapel out, because who else is going to come all the way up here to clean it. . .?' The only thing is, I forgot to bring oil and a wick, to light the lamp. . . Never mind – next time. I really hadn't believed grandma, with her story about the seaweed. I pushed open the little wooden door and went in. I almost fell over from the shock. The whole chapel smelt of sea and seaweed. I knew that smell. The seaweed was about a foot deep. I reached down and picked up a handful. It was long, and grey-brown in colour. The weed was still wet from the sea. How on earth could seaweed have found its way to the mountains of Thessaly. . .? And still wet, too. . .

It was everywhere – in the choir-stall, on the candelabra,

some hanging in the pews, and some on the candle-stall. There were even two starfish – live ones! I fell to my knees and cried and cried...! I don't know why... Because I hadn't believed grandma's stories about St Nicholas and his journeys? No...! My crying had a happiness in it, as if I had found something that I had lost... The sea... and seaweed... and St Nicholas... I thought of the saint travelling over the foaming waters and calming them with one finger, and the waves falling quiet, like children when they go to sleep. How tired the saint would be... How many seas he would have calmed. How many pieces of seaweed he would have shaken from his clothes... And later on, tired from having saved so many lives and so many sailing boats, he would have returned to his icon and slept.

After a while I got up. I gathered the seaweed and made a pile of it outside, near the parapet. I put rocks on it to stop it blowing about. There was oil in the little bottle. Only about an inch, but it was enough. I went out. Surely I must be able to find some wicks around the chapel, somewhere. In the end I found one. I lit the oil lamp. It was really old. And dusty. I rubbed it and rubbed it on my skirt till it shone. It was made of bronze and inset with red stones. Hanging below, it had a cross which was also made of red stones. The eyes of the saint followed me, watching everything I did and everywhere I went. I fell to my knees and prayed harder than I had ever prayed before. For my daughter, mainly.

I came out again feeling as light as air. 'Bless you, grandma,' I thought, 'for sending me here.' A light breeze was blowing, and it brought a slight tinkling noise to my ears. It couldn't have been sheep's bells. I turned the bend in the road and saw the Tree in the distance. It was a huge oak tree. Three grown men wouldn't have been able to encircle it. It was a proud, free-standing oak. And as I thought this I suddenly froze. It was the 'lone oak tree' that the strange woman had talked about. 'You must listen to the leaves of the lone oak,' she had told me. But here, among the leaves, shone strange little things. I went closer. They were round metal trinkets. They were not easy to see up amongst the leaves, but some had fallen to the ground. Some were long and thin. Whoever had made them had also carved lines around them, and written on them. Our kind of lettering, so I could read it. On one of them it said 'Vanity, vanity, all is vanity'. Another one – a round one – said: 'Moderation in all things.' Then there was 'When the fox can't reach the grapes, he says they're sour', and 'The world goes round', and 'Fire, woman, and sea', and 'Know thyself', and 'People who don't enjoy life should die, because they don't deserve the space they take up in this world', and 'Listen, watch, and be silent'. I picked up some of the trinkets and put them in my pocket. I would ask grandma about them later. First I was going to wash in the stream. There wasn't a soul about. Only the oak, the spring, and myself. I undressed, I washed myself all over, I gave my hair a good soaking, and I drank some of the water. It tasted good. . . like holy water! It had a taste, a scent like lavender, or laurel. . . I began to feel dizzy. . . Especially since I hadn't eaten all day. I dressed and stood up. I wasn't feeling well. As though I was tired, or about to faint. I thought: 'I'll stop off under the Tree, for a rest, and then I'll go back down.' I lay down between its roots. They came out of the ground like great arms. Above me the leaves on the Tree were moving, and the trinkets were sparkling with a thousand flashing lights as the sun fell on them. The leaves of the Tree were whispering, talking to each other, but I didn't understand a word. The strange woman had told me quite specifically, though: 'You must listen to the leaves of the lone oak tree.' I closed my eyes and listened. But I couldn't hear a thing. Nothing! It was as if the wind had dropped completely, and not a leaf moved. I was annoyed with myself for believing an old wives' tale.

I almost shouted at the Tree: 'Tell me... Shall I find my Persephone...?' Silence. Not a sound. Not even the tinkling.

'Why do you torment me...? You *can't* speak – that's it, isn't it...! Talking trees, indeed! Trees don't talk...! And here I sit, like an idiot, talking with you, and waiting...!'

And before I could say '...for an answer', all of a sudden a wind blew up. I still shudder at the thought of it, more than sixty years later. The Tree shook its branches angrily, and snorted, and its leaves rustled and roared...

I was frozen with fear. A lump in my throat made me cough. I coughed and coughed... My fingers were trembling and I thought I was going to wet myself... Then, all of a sudden, words started coming out of my mouth. As if of their own accord:

Today you lie, as a fruitful
many-branched olive tree lies,
uprooted by the violent blowing
of harsh winds...

What did these words mean...? Had *I* spoken them...? Or was it the leaves of the Tree...? But how can leaves speak...? And then again, I don't say those kinds of words... I couldn't... But they came out of my mouth, of their own accord... The way you sometimes speak your thoughts out loud, without realizing it...? That's right – but how could I have said words that I didn't even know...? Was it the leaves, maybe...? I didn't know what to think.

I set off on my way back down. I stopped at the round stones again and looked at the letters. A thought had crossed my mind. Not that I believed it – it was just a thought. I remembered the things that we used to say when we were children: 'If it's time for daddy to come with a present, let the cat sneeze,' or 'If there are two lines on the cobblestones, I lose; if there's only one, I win. . .' The sort of games you played on your own. And now here I was, grown-up, and saying to myself: 'If the Tree really did speak to me, I shall be able to read the ancient letters on the stones.'

Impossible, I thought. Cannot be. . . Anyway, I stopped at the stones, and I was sure that I wouldn't be able to read them.

'ALOS' it said, clear as day. 'ALOS' In other words, the ancient Greek for *aloni* – threshing floor.

'I can hear you're out of breath, my girl. Have you been running?' grandma said, and nodded to me to come closer.

I couldn't say a thing. I was so tired. My legs were like lead. I collapsed onto a chair.

'I found the seaweed and I swept it up. I found these trinkets too, under the Tree.'

Grandma laughed with joy.

'My man made them. He used to make them when he came home after work. . . At first just for fun, but later because he couldn't stop himself. He had to carve these trinkets. He would cut them, make patterns on them, write sayings on them and the date, and then hang them on the Tree. To teach the children. And to give us all something to think about. In those days, everyone used to meet around the Tree. They would drink water from the spring. They would sit on the threshing floor. . . Later the Church forbade it. . .'

'Grandma,' I said, 'don't laugh. . . Please. . . The Tree. . . I think it talked to me. . . How could it. . .? Could a tree talk. . .?'

'Hmm. . . That isn't just any old tree, it's *the* Tree. It has always spoken. . . Only to women, mind you! They used to visit the Tree without the priest knowing. They would bathe and drink some water, and then they would ask their questions. To some women the Tree would speak, and to others not. It has never spoken to me. I'd do what you were supposed to do, but it never did speak. . . Did you say it spoke to you? Are you sure. . .? It is both a blessing and a curse for the Tree to speak to you. It can be a great burden. Some women were able to carry it, but others went crazy. Some of them ran down into the ravine like mad women. Their husbands would tie them up, the priest would come to exorcize them, but their minds had gone. The Tree hasn't spoken for years now, though. You say it spoke to you. . .? Are you sure. . .? You have to fast for three days, and wash yourself in running water, and drink three mouthfuls of water, and then lie down with your feet facing the East. Then ask the Tree your question, quietly, and it will answer you. If it wishes. Not if it *can*. . . If it *wants* to. . .! If it feels you are strong enough to hear. . .'

From that day, the Tree spoke to me many times. And later on it spoke to Eleni too.

ROULA

Stupid damn place. Nobody tells you anything and nobody knows anything. It's all, 'Yes. . . Well, maybe. . . but then again maybe not. . .'

I asked them: 'Can you tell me the time of the next bus to Rizes?'

The only answer I got was: 'Let's see. If there are enough people for Tyrnavo, then you'll get away tonight. Otherwise you'll have to take the morning bus for Elassona.'

'And when can I get a through bus to Rizes?'

'There isn't one. You have to go via Tyrnavo or Elassona.'

The bus for Tyrnavo filled up, and we set off. I thought it

would take a couple of hours at least, and that we'd be going up mountains. Where I got that idea from, I don't know. Fifteen minutes later we were in Tyrnavo. The conductor said I'd have to spend the night there, or take a taxi. The taxi would take me as far as the crossroads, and I'd have to walk the rest of the way.

I wasn't wild at the prospect of spending a night in a hotel in Tyrnavo, being eaten alive by bugs. The taxi to the crossroads would cost me three hundred drachmas. That was as far as it went. It'd be along in about an hour. Someone had cut his hand, and the taxi driver had had to run him to hospital in Larisa. There were other taxis in town, but they told me that Tassos was the only one who did the crossroads run. Oh well. Whatever will be will be! At least I've only got a small Adidas bag with me. I got incredibly thirsty on that damn bus from Athens. The driver decided to stop for a meal-break at Kammena Vourla, without so much as a by-your-leave. Who wants to eat lunch at eleven in the morning?! I had some cold macaroni, and a warm beer, and paid a small fortune for the pleasure. Now I'm going to a café for a tsibouro, the local drink. That's what Antonis told me: 'Make sure you stop off for a tsibouro if you're going to Tyrnavo, otherwise you'll be missing something.' An arsehole of a place, this Tyrnavo! A small town square, with all the usual shops. A greengrocer's, strings of garlic hanging up, and red peppers and yellow marrows. I went into a café. It was tiny, but there was still room for ten tables. Small round tables they were, with black chairs, and not a soul in the place at that time of day. Well there wouldn't be, would there! I mean, who wants to drink tsibouro at five in the afternoon! Nobody except me, and I was only there because I was doing the tourist bit. So that I could go back to the office and say 'I had a tsibouro in Tyrnavo.' I went up to the man behind the counter and said: 'A tsibouro, please.' Then I went and sat down. I was expecting a small glass and a couple of olives, and then I'd be on my way. Not a bit of it! He brought: a small carafe of tsibouro, aubergine salad, stuffed aubergines with pickle, pickled cabbage, fried red peppers, crayfish – yes, really, crayfish – and fried courgettes.

'I asked for a drink,' I said, 'not a bloody banquet.'

He explained that this was the usual meze they served. Then he sat down and started telling me how he'd prepared each of the dishes. Even the crayfish were local, he said, from the big stone troughs down where the streams run into the river. I was on the point of saying, 'Well... that's really amazing...!' but I restrained myself. I decided to be ladylike. He asked me where I was from. 'Athens,' I replied. And what was my job? 'Journalist.' (Put it this way, if you can't act flash in Tyrnavo, then where *can* you act flash...?) When he heard the word journalist, he started to get all excited. He got up without a word, went behind the counter, and brought me some more crayfish. Then he went out, and came back with some old fogey. The old fogey was wearing a silver-coloured tie, a dirty shirt and a hat. He took his hat off and, can you believe it, he kissed my hand...! (Which, by this time, stank of crayfish...)

'What an honour for our town,' he said, 'to be host to a journalist from Athens. And for yours truly what an honour to be speaking to you. Of course, the spheres of cultured folk are bound to intersect, whether they're from Athens or Tyrnavo. I have often admired you on television.' (At this point my jaw must have dropped in amazement.) 'I shall be eternally grateful to Argyris for having informed me that you were here...'

He looked at me, his little eyes flitting right and left. The man's obviously ready for the mad-house, I thought. Senile dementia. I was about to disabuse him, but then I changed my mind. The penny dropped. The old creep was under the illusion that I was the journalist Liana Kanelli. Which was not surprising, because that's who I looked like. I'd told my hairdresser to do my hair just like hers. It turned out brilliantly. And when I made up my eyebrows, and looked a bit wide-eyed when I talked to people, and hung a little cross on a chain round my neck, I really looked like her. The only thing I couldn't manage was the voice. I got it down as low as I could, but it wasn't far enough. It came out sounding pretty streetwise, but not like Kanelli's. I missed that lady when they sacked her. . . A lot of people phoned and wrote to the papers, to get her job back, but it didn't do any good.

'Will you be staying for a while, Miss Liana, or are you passing through?' the old man asked.

'I'm on my way to Rizes – I have to leave shortly.'

'You reporters are always on the go, eh. . .! Well, journalism is a way of life I suppose. . . Of course, I appreciate that. Whatever the effort, whatever the difficulty, nothing is allowed to stand in the way of a good story. . . You know, our town of Tyrnavo has a thousand problems. . . and. . .'

I realized what he was getting at, and I said to myself: 'Miss Kanelli – time to make a move! This is not for us. Time to make ourselves scarce before they catch on.'

The old chap who ran the shop was refusing to accept my money, and the old fogey was insisting on paying for me, so one way and another I got off scot free. 'Here's to you, Liana baby!' I muttered, as I downed the last of the tsibouro.

By the time I left the place, I was flying. You wouldn't think a few tsibouros would do your head in, but I could already feel the hangover coming on.

I went and sat at the back of the taxi rank, in front of a gloomy little shop. There was a chair outside. I decided I'd better sit down and sober up a bit, so as not to make a fool of myself in the cab. I put down my Adidas bag and lit a cigarette. I'd hardly taken a puff when out popped an old lady

with a chair. She put it next to me and looked at me. I looked
at her in turn, and said:

'Good evening.'

'Welcome. Are you from here?'

'No. I'm from Athens.'

The old lady didn't say another word. She just gazed into
the distance. What was she looking at, for God's sake! But it
was just as well, really, because all these old people were
starting to get on my nerves. Not to mention the thought of
all the relations I was about to meet...

The taxi driver was fine. He arrived when he was supposed to,
and off we went. He told me he would take the middle road
from Tyrnavo, the one that went towards Elassona. He'd
drop me off in about twelve kilometres, and I'd have to walk
the rest of the way.

'Is it far from the crossroads?' I asked.

'A fair distance, especially if you're not used to it... But if
you wait for a while, you usually find there's a tractor going
up. They come back from the fields at about this time.'

'But how long's it going to take me if I end up having to
walk?' I asked.

'Half an hour. Forty-five minutes, maybe... It's uphill, you
see.'

It didn't take long to get to the crossroads, because most of
the journey was across a plain. It was only at the end that it
started going uphill. In the fields, they were burning the dry
maize stalks, and harvesting the grapes too.

'Those are the late grapes,' the driver told me. 'They're the
ones that make the best wine in Tyrnavo.'

(To hell with Tyrnavo wines – I was more concerned about
the prospect of having to walk up that hill.)

'Mr Tassos,' I said, as sweetly as I could, 'is there any
chance you could run me up to the village...?'

'Out of the question, mademoiselle,' he said. 'I happen to be attached to my car. The only thing that would get up there is a tractor, or maybe a jeep. It's a dirt road, with rocks all the way. So don't even ask. . .'

I was furious. Up yours too, you stupid old peasant – you've only got an old wreck anyway. . . Then I watched him drive off, and I looked at the mountain on my right. I was furious. What was I supposed to do now. . . Out of the frying pan into the fire. . . I could have kicked myself. . . you idiot, I thought. . . You could have been sitting in a nice bar on Fokionos Negri street, but instead here you are, stuck like an idiot at the arse end of Thessaly. I should never have promised. . . But so what, anyway. . .? Mrs Archontoula is hardly going to punish me if I don't go. You know. . . What the hell, though, I'm doing it for myself, really. I said I'd do it, and so I'm doing it. Not because of my Mum, and not because of a promise. Right, girl, pick up your bag and let's get going . . .

You know what, it's really pretty up here. Woods and trees on both sides of the road. I'm not too sure what sort of trees – pines, or maybe plane trees . . .? There are streams, too. It's turning a bit chilly. I'd better put my jacket on.

As I was standing there, buttoning up my coat, I heard the sound of an engine. A tractor was coming up. 'Struck lucky again,' I thought. I waited till it reached me, and asked the driver if he was going on up. He stopped about ten yards beyond me, as if he'd had to think about it first.

'Are you going to Rizes?'

He nodded to me to climb up. It's not so easy getting up on a tractor. The step's really high. I held on to the handrail for dear life, and with a jolt we were off.

'Whose daughter are you?' the old fellow asked.

I was about to say, 'I'm my mother's and my father's' but after all he had just saved me from a long walk uphill. . .

'I'm going to Mrs Dimitra Chatsiphoti's,' I said.

The old man opened his jacket, spat three times, and crossed himself. . . Mother of God, what kind of behaviour is that?!

'My uncle Fotos has died. That's why I've come. . .'

Why the hell was I trying to justify myself. . .? Fuck off, you useless old pig! Why had he spat three times and crossed himself. . .? I was furious. If he asks any more questions, I thought, I'm not saying a word.

As it happened, he didn't ask. He didn't say a word, in fact. Didn't even look at me. Just as well. But then it started raining, and he opened up a black umbrella and passed it to me. I thought of leaving him out of it so's he'd get soaked, but then I felt sorry for him, so I held it over him too.

We reached the village. There was a small church in the square, and a spring that was spouting water out of a lion's mouth. The clock on the church tower stood at five to twelve. My watch said seven-twenty.

'The church clock's stopped. . .?' I said, by way of conversation.

'Years ago,' he said.

So you even grudge me a couple of words, you old fucker, eh? Why? What have I ever done to you. . .? Don't tell me – I trod on your corns. . .! I warn you – I was really getting annoyed by then.

We stopped outside a house. At the door stood an old lady, wearing a white headscarf and an apron.

'Whose daughter are you, my dear?' she asked.

'Don't worry about that,' the man said. ' I'll tell you later.' She went quiet. But her eyes were like flies walking all over me. . . searching, searching. . .

I found the road that the old man told me to take. The damn road was all slippery underfoot. I must have been soft in the head to wear my clogs, clattering about on this road. I should have worn my espadrilles or my trainers. Anyway, what the hell... Come on, let's find the house and the old lady and get it over with. He said the first house has an anchor outside it. An anchor! I ask you! Peculiar habits around here. Nobody lives in the house any more, the man said. He gave me directions, told me to carry on, and follow the little wall until I came to another little house. Come on, let's get on with it. Apart from anything else, I'm bursting...

ELENI

Footsteps. I wonder if it's our Archontoula...? Let's have a look. No – it's a stranger. She's wearing trousers, too... Mind you, she's coming towards the house... I wonder why. She must be lost. This road doesn't lead anywhere else. It only leads to our house... She's carrying an overnight bag... I wonder if it's one of Archontoula's friends, come to tell us that she can't come...? Holy Mary...! The woman's the image of Archontoula when she was young...! Who on earth can she be...? Archontoula's daughter...? And what about our Archontoula...? Where is our Archontoula? Is she ill, or something? Why hasn't she come...?

ROULA

I'm exhausted, damn it. Almost there, though. That's the little house. The old lady must be potty about flowers. It's hardly a house, really... more like a cabin. In fact, it looks more more like Karagiozis's shack. It's smothered in flowers. No idea what they're called, though. Clay pots and even old tin cans used as flower pots; and there's even a broken children's swing.

There's an old lady at the door. I wonder if that's my mother's mother? God, how am I going to start calling her 'granny'... 'old lady' is what springs to mind. 'Granny' is what I call my next-door neighbour in Kypseli... It's bound to slip out, though... I'll call my grandma 'old lady' and there'll be hell to pay.

No, that can't be her. She's about the same age as my mother would have been. The old lady – my 'granny' – must have been about twenty when she had my mother? Something like that. So by now she must be at least eighty, give or take a bit. And still going strong. Healthy bones, these old timers. Well obviously, my dear – they don't smoke... they're not forced to eat chicken fed with hormones... or artificially ripened tomatoes... And they don't have to put up with pollution either. Credit where credit's due... this might be the arsehole of the world, no shops, and all that, but at least the place is bursting with fresh air...

I tell you, that old lady's got eyes like a hawk... If you ask me, she doesn't like the look of me, but why should I worry? I'm doing my duty...

'I'm looking for Mrs Dimitra Chatsiphoti...' For God's sake, why doesn't she say something, instead of just staring at me like she's seen a ghost.

'I'm the daughter of Archontoula, the daughter of...'

'Child...'

The old woman's started crying. Don't cry, for God's sake, we'll have enough of that at the funeral... And don't start hugging and kissing me either, because I hate that sort of thing. Who the hell is this woman...?

And who's this other one, coming out of the house...? Absolute picture of health: blonde hair... and clear blue eyes. She's standing in front of me, and she's looking at me... The way she stands, it's as if she can't actually see me...

'It's my Archontoula. . .?'

That's all she says. . .

I suppose this must be her. My mother's mother. My 'granny'. How am I going to tell her that her daughter's died? The shock could kill her.

MOTHER

So my Archontoula's dead, too. . . Another one of my babies gone. . . Went with a bad heart, poor thing. And she died so young. She still had years ahead of her, my Archontoula.

I had Archontoula after I'd had Persephone and the twins. It was an easy birth. I was digging the garden to plant some cabbages when my labour pains started. I remembered my grandmother's advice – God bless her – and I squatted as if I was going to pass water. I strained and strained, and out she came. As easy as that. I cut the belly-cord with a clean, sharpened reed. The things that field has seen. . .!

At some point I spent a month at grandma's. The weather had taken a turn for the worst. That was in November 1923. While we were staying with grandma, I did the cooking and fed her, and she told me stories. That morning I was feeling very restless. For no particular reason. This used to happen to me a lot. I decided to go and ask the Tree about it the next day. Every time I felt this lump in my throat and this shivering in my belly, I felt the need to visit the Tree. I would fast and then I would go.

That morning, at about eleven, a lad came up from the bottom house and brought some goat's meat for us and a bit of food for the man who was ploughing the field down below. He hadn't bothered to shut grandma's front door, and a bolt of lightning suddenly hit the house. If it had hit the child, it would have killed him outright. He started crying his eyes out. We tried to console him, but it was no good. By then it was raining cats and dogs... When the rain eased up, grandma told him to take the man his food, because he'd been working since dawn and he'd be hungry. There was no way of shifting the boy, though; he was too scared to go out. Grandma took him in her arms and rocked him gently. He quietened down, and began sucking his thumb and rocking himself. In a little while he was fast asleep. Is there anything sweeter than the sight of a young child sleeping? Even the naughtiest child looks like an angel. Then grandma told me to take the food to the man, because he'd be getting angry, and before you knew it he'd be getting drunk and starting a scene. I took the food, and an umbrella, and out I went. I used to like walking in the rain. The ground had a strong smell of rotting leaves. There'd been a lot of rain. Here and there my feet got stuck in the mud. I saw him from a distance. He was ploughing the field in the rain. It was the first time this field of grandma's had been sown for years.

'I've finished,' he said to me. 'I've ploughed it three times now.'

After the third ploughing they used to stop and sow.

It was in that thrice ploughed field that the man took me for the first time. By force. I tried struggling, but he was too strong for me. With one push he threw me to the ground. I could feel my back getting soaked and my feet getting filthy with the mud. I struggled to get up to throw some mud in his face, but it was no good. I closed my eyes, shut my mouth tight, and prayed to God to save me. Nothing. He came into me. He was silent at first, and then he started groaning. I was in pain. I didn't want him. I loathed him. He was just about to finish when he ripped my blouse in his frenzy. He saw Andronikos's picture, and stopped. He looked at me, and then looked at the picture, without a word. And then he started again. More brutally than before. He was talking filth and shouting 'whore' at me. I was crying. I was still crying when he finished and got up. I stayed on the ground. Lost.

He picked up a flask and drank some wine from it. He laughed and said: 'This field will be the most fertile of all.'

And so it was. Both the field and me. Nine months later I gave birth to the twins. My Fotos and my Eleni. Grandma helped me at the birth.

We put up some boards from her double bed and spread some old torn sheets on them. I was having a very hard time. My belly was very big, and the July heat was a torment. I didn't go out, in case anyone saw me. Only when it was cool in the evenings could I go out into the little yard and sit on the parapet. The child was moving inside my belly. It was moving differently to when I'd had Persephone, but I told myself that it was just the passing of the years. It was kicking on two sides at once. I was scared that it would turn out to be an idiot child, because that man had also taken me during my pregnancy. He used to come into my grandma's house, grab me, and drag me to the shed. He'd take me right there, among the pitchforks and hoes, as if I was an animal. Grandma would cry and plead with him, saying that I was a woman in distress, and that it wasn't right, and that he would pay for it in the end. But he ignored her.

One day his mother came up as well. Despinio. She was a hard-hearted, miserable woman. She looked about fifty, but later I learned she was only forty-three. They'd married her off at fifteen. At sixteen she had had her first child. She gave me a long hard look, saw how big my belly was getting, and spat hard words at me: 'You can take your little bastard and go, you dirty refugee bitch. I know your kind, you scum. Make sure you're out by tomorrow.'

She had this grudge against the refugees, because she'd lost her husband, Thodoros, in the Smyrna disaster in 1922.

And we who had come from Asia Minor were to blame...
But we'd lost our families too. I'd lost Andronikos, and my
Persephone. So many people dead in Asia Minor...

I didn't have to leave, though, thanks to grandma. She had a
big argument with Despinio, and said that the house was
hers, and as long as she was alive, I could live there too.

I stayed, and I had the twins there. Fotos came first, and
Eleni came six hours later. Grandma took the babies. It was
she who washed them. It was she who put the babies to my
breast – one on each nipple. She was like a little girl in her
happiness. Even though she couldn't see, she did everything
that was needed. She put the afterbirth in a clay pot and left it
somewhere – she said it was so the snake of the house could
eat it. And she did something else too. She signed over her
garden to me, and her shed – the storage place. She told the
priest who had come to give her communion.

'The house is for them – the others, I mean – but the
garden and the shed are for the orphans.'

Grandma never called them 'bastards'. She'd always say 'the
orphans'.

On the day of Epiphany 1925, she died. She was a hundred
and eighteen years old. I was pregnant again. With
Archontoula.

ELENI

She looks like our Archontoula. Except that she wears
trousers. And her hair has strange light streaks in it. Look at
her now; she's taken her shoes off and she's smoking a
cigarette. It's not right. Here only the men smoke, and then
not in front of their mothers. And they call her Roula! Not

Dimitra, but Roula. . .! I suppose it's the same with us – after all, they call Thodoroula's daughter Ritsa at home. Anyway, Roula has kept the promise she made to her mother, Archontoula, and she's come. Everyone's made differently. Who knows, maybe in Athens all the women dress like this. . . and smoke too. . .

How could Archontoula stand to live in Athens, though? She was used to different ways. A good housewife, a hard worker, and not a lot to say for herself. Out of all of us, she was the weakest. She was very slight, compared with the rest of us. Thodoroula and Despo, and myself as well, we all turned out giants.

People always used to think that I was strong. How wrong they were. . .! I'm like a twig on the ocean. . . Nobody ever imagines how much I've suffered. Because this 'thing' that makes me suffer has its own laws. It comes up all of a sudden. One minute I'm thinking, 'Thanks be to God, I'm all right', and the next I'm shouting, 'Mother of God, help me!' I never have any warning. . . it just comes over me suddenly. And after what happened I never married, never felt the love of a man. . . My mother was getting me ready for the Tree. She told me so, but I made up all kinds of stories, in the hope that something might happen and I might escape. Because Lambraina's son Yannis was making eyes at me. And I loved him in return. We'd never exchanged a word, but we both used to take our goats to the same place. We used to look at each other. I had such sweet feelings when we looked at each other.

I was still young when I first saw blood on my legs. It was a trickle of blood that ran down and reached my knee. I was scared. 'It' had got a hold of me. I ran out of the house. In the opposite direction to usual. I lost myself deep in the forest. I found some water and washed myself to get rid of the blood.

But then more blood came. I wasn't afraid about the blood so much. . . I was scared because I loved Yannis and I wanted to marry him. And if I went to the Tree, then I would have to love nobody but the Tree. No man would be permitted to touch me.

That night I slept in the forest. A restless, uneasy sleep. I felt as if eyes were watching me from all sides. In the morning I found a garland of ivy and vine-leaves lying next to me. I placed it on my head. All day I wandered in the forest. I was talking to myself. I didn't want to go back home. I didn't want to go to the Tree.

The second night, I heard a man's voice. He was calling my name. I was frightened, and climbed up into a willow tree. I stayed there all night. I thought I saw a man with curly hair and horns. . .

He didn't come the next evening, but I slept up in the willow tree just in case. While I was asleep, I had a strange dream. It made me scared for my family – for my mother and my brothers and sisters. But I had to. . . I had to go to the Tree. Even if I didn't want to.

When I returned home, my mother took me there. I was clean by then.

And as the years passed, I made a decision. This was the way I would be – I would never marry. . .

Archontoula used to be a wonderful weaver. . .! Really wonderful. . .! She used to weave beautiful, delicate sheets. . . Mother wouldn't let her till the fields or tend the sheep. She only worked in the house, cooking, weaving and looking after the little ones. We each had our jobs. Fotos and I looked after the sheep. My mother and Thodoroula saw to the fields. And the little ones – Tassos, Yannis and Despo – all had their jobs in the house. Those were hard times – very hard. We didn't expect anything from *him*. He was a passing stranger.

Eight children he'd made with our mother, and never a thought for how they'd grow up. Everything was left to mother.

She planted that garden of grandma Maria – may the earth that covers her be light – and she turned it into a paradise. There was everything you could wish for. Once a week, Fotos went down to the market at Larisa to sell our produce. The local villagers wouldn't buy from us. They were afraid. Partly because of my mother's strange ways and my habits, and partly because of Despinio's threats. That's why they didn't want to see us. Despinio – my grandmother, that is – used to walk on the other side when she saw us. And so we too got in the habit of taking different routes. And they abandoned grandma Maria's house – the one with the anchor that they'd inherited – and it went to ruin. The ceilings fell in, the roof fell in, everything went... And why? So that Despinio need not see us. Evil woman. And she made her children that way too. Crabbed and miserly. The only one who was different was her son, my uncle Yannis. He was very young when he married my aunt Pagona, and they went to live in Tyrnavo. He was the only one who came to see us – but he had to come secretly, without his mother knowing, and he used to bring us things when he came to visit.

We saw him shortly before he was killed, in 1942. There were fifteen of them from Tyrnavo. They fell into a German trap and they were killed. His wife, Pagona, was killed too. His is the fifth garment in the collection, a wedding suit. We shall have to get these clothes ready now, in time. I'll need my brothers and sisters to come and give a hand. Thodoroula can come straight away. She only lives a little way out of the village. An outsider came to ask for her hand – a carpenter by trade – and he married her. It didn't worry him that she was a bastard and had no dowry. They have a good life together. They have three children – Ritsa and two boys. Then Tassos and our Despo left to go to Larisa. They'd got on well together, ever since they were children. First Tassos went to Larisa, and then he took Despo as well. They found work in Larisa, in the flour mills. Despo married a tailor, a good, sweet-natured man. But they never had any children, and this was a great sorrow to them. Tassos married too, and now he has two sons. I shall have to get word to them, our brother and sister in Larisa.

ROULA

The old lady's frowning at me because I'm smoking. Not my granny. . . the other old lady. . . my 'auntie'. My mum certainly had a big family! But she only ever talked about Fotos. I wonder why. . .?

I saw him there, lying there, looking like he was dead to the world. But in fact he was alive. Not at all like someone who's at death's door. And I've only got three days' off from work.

My boss was pretty ratty when I phoned. I explained the whole business in detail, and told him I'd be late getting back. What was I supposed to do? You can't just ignore death and carry on like everything's normal.

Anyway, if he hasn't popped off within three or four days, I've decided I'm leaving. You won't see me for dust. There's not even anywhere to stay round here. Not a hotel in sight. A bit thin on creature comforts, you might say. I mean, it's clean, but definitely primitive. . . When I wanted a wash, I had to get water from the little tank on the wall, one of those pre-war zinc efforts, with the picture of the shepherdesses.

The bed's hard – you'd be better off sleeping on the floor. Then there's my aunt – she's put a cheap rug down and she's sleeping on that. And the old lady, my 'granny', keeps getting up in the middle of the night because she can't sleep. She starts rummaging around the house. They've got a cupboard with drawers and she opens it up and starts hunting through them. In the end I couldn't stand it any longer and shouted, 'Keep quiet!' And what about waking up in the morning?! I leapt up – because it felt like some bloody insect was walking on my face, and I can't stand insects – and what did I find? The old lady – my 'granny' – was sitting there stroking my face. She frightened the life out of me! They're a weird bunch, these women. Why can't uncle just die quietly, so's we can get it over with. I mean, what am I supposed to do stuck in a dump like this? We're not even anywhere near the village. . . . So I sit outside on the wall and smoke a cigarette and drink my coffee.

I spoke too soon, saying that uncle was relaxed. He suddenly started yelling (I nearly fainted) and tried to get up. The two old ladies tried to hold him down, but they couldn't. And he was shouting, over and over again, 'Archontoula, Archontoula!'

Shit – this is taking things too far. I must have been crazy to want to come. It was different when my mum died. She died peacefully, not like this. Luckily, she wasn't in pain. With her second heart attack, that is. Because with the first one she spent two months in hospital.

They had to stick her in a camp bed out in the corridor, and even the corridor was full to overflowing. They fixed her up with a drip in her arm and a catheter. An 'acute pulmonary oedema and a cardiovascular infarct', that's what they said it was. All evening I used to sit looking into her eyes, thinking, 'Don't die without me noticing.' Sometimes she would shut her eyes and then I'd get up and listen to her breathing. She couldn't sleep, though – despite all the injections. It was as if she was scared. Then she'd open her eyes and nod to me, as if to say, 'I'm all right.' When they finally had a bed in intensive care, they took her in. I would sleep there at nights, sometimes on a stretcher in the corridor and sometimes on two chairs put together. There were others there too. A young headmistress; a rich woman with blonde hair; three brothers... Every time the ward door opened, we would all jump up. We knew what it meant... Somebody was in danger...! We'd all run to the door and make nervous inquiries about own own relatives. After all... Later on, they put her in a single room. If you didn't have somebody there to look after you, you were done for. One day they tried to give mum a cream pudding, even though she suffered from diabetes. Anyway, when the doctors told me she had no more than a year to live, I told her I'd bring her in some cakes, in secret, her favourites. But she was so scared of the doctors that she said no.

She was terrified of the doctors. She suffered years of torment because of them – the diabetes, her heart, her circulation. And the pigs knew her days were numbered, but they still tried to persuade her to have another examination – catheterization, they called it. Utter torture. My mother knew what the pain would be like – everyone talked about it in the ward – and she refused.

'I shall die of fear in the lift,' she told them, 'when you take me up for examination.'

Those bastards. They were giving her one test after another. Until I got angry and started shouting:

'Why are you upsetting her?' I asked them. 'What good are tests going to do her? You're not going to operate, are you? Because the woman doesn't want it. So why are you tormenting her?'

They're just sadists.

The second time, nothing helped her, not even calling an

ambulance. We'd brought her down to the steps outside the flats so she could be ready.

At Athena's house they were having a party. It was the last Saturday of Carnival. I would have gone too, but my mother hadn't slept so well the night before. It was only when I made the promise about Fotos that she calmed down and went to sleep. A little before midnight she said she was feeling bad and wanted to get up.

I knocked at Athena's, next door, because Takis, her husband, is a doctor. Well, he's a radiologist really, but he knows about these things. He understood. We rang for an ambulance. Sophia's husband, Dimitri, ran to find a chemist's that was open. He scoured the whole of Kypseli, and when he returned proudly with her injection – adrenalin they called it, I think – we no longer needed it. Archontoula was already gone.

You've never seen a sadder clown than Dimitri that night. He was wearing a clown costume, and a big painted grin, and a spotty tie, and braces and so on. He should have looked really comical, but he looked sort of frozen as he stood there with the injection. He was crying, too, I think.

I never walk on that bit of the stairs where my mother died.

Come on, Roula, pull yourself together. Now we've got another death to deal with.

MOTHER

Fotos is calling my Archontoula's name again. What are we to do. . .? This granddaughter of mine is so strange. Not just because she's never come to visit us. . . No, she's just strange. She doesn't seem to care about us, or about our Fotos. . .

When I told her that she should answer when he calls 'Archontoula', she gave me a long look and then shrugged, as if to say: 'You're crazy. . .!' I explained to her that in order for Fotos to be at peace, I wanted her to pretend to be her mother, Archontoula. So that he can tell her what it is he has to tell her, and she can answer as if she's Archontoula, in order for my Fotos to find repose. Because Fotos did what he did for Archontoula's sake. . .

It was the spring of 1942. The end of spring. We had a lot of work in the sheepfold, because we were cheese-making. I was doing things I had not done since I was a child. I used to get up at four in the morning, as the sun was coming up, and I'd take the animals out to pasture. When I got back, Fotos would be milking and then Eleni would churn the sheep's milk for me. Then they used to wake the younger children, so that Archontoula could look after them. That particular day I went up high, up to the Tree, to find a little pasture for the sheep, and to try and gather my wits a bit, because I'd woken in a very bad mood. I'd had a dream which felt like some sort of omen, though I could not understand it at the time.

It went like this: the Sky had come down to earth – like a man made of thick black cloud. He had sex with me – raped me – all night long. When the morning came I began giving birth to children – many children – but he – that's to say, the Sky – hid them in a secret place, and I couldn't find them. I was very worried for my children, and I hated the Sky – the man who had hidden them from me. Then I took a sickle with a sharp blade and I gave it to a large boy – like a giant – one of the children I still had with me. 'Ah, my boy,' I asked him, 'do you want to punish your father for the bad way he's treated you? It was he who thought up this dirty business.' The child said, 'Mother, I make you a promise. I care nothing for our father. I hate his very name. As you say, he thought up this dirty business.' I was glad. I hid the child. I gave him the sickle and I told him the plan. When the Sky came again that night, he embraced me and lay on top of me. Then my son grabbed hold of him with his left hand, and with his right hand, which held the sickle, he cut off his father's testicles. I gathered Sky's blood as it fell, and I gave birth to some girls, who were born old, with snakes in place of hair. I hurled his testicles into the sea, and all at once a very beautiful girl was born. The Sky did not return to my bed. This was my dream.

It's true. The Sky in the dream and *he* are very similar. That's the way *he* always used to take me – by force. I hated him, but what could I do? When my first two children were born – the twins, Fotos and Eleni – I should have just taken them and run away. But where could I have gone – a woman on her own, with two babies...? And then there was the strange fact that my Eleni was born with a small cross on her shoulder. It was like a mole, but it was blue, like my Persephone's little cross. I thought that it was God's will that I should stay here, and that my Eleni and my Persephone were both here with me. *He* never spared a thought for us, or for his children. In the last years he only ever came up to our cabin when he wanted a woman. He was good for nothing. The children and I had to struggle, hanging on by our teeth, to survive. My Fotos and Eleni were eighteen by then, and Archontoula was sixteen.

When he heard Archontoula's screams, Fotos came running in. Partly because he was close by the house at that moment, and partly because Archontoula was screaming, 'Save me, brother Fotos, save me.'

Fotos had been sharpening sickles on the whetstone, for the harvest was about to begin. He ran in, holding one of them. That's what he killed him with. The anti-Christ had coveted his own daughter – my Archontoula.

My Eleni came up to the pasture. She was out of breath, and her eyes were staring. She told me. And I, poor wretch, came running back like a mad woman. Not because of *him* – may the earth that covers him be like lead – but for my children. The young ones were out with the rabbits; Thodoroula, who was grown-up, had gone to get water from grandma's cistern. Only Fotos and Eleni were there. We bundled him up and hid him among the sheep, and in the evening Fotos went and buried him somewhere. The next day I got up at dawn, but Archontoula had gone. Ten years later she sent me a letter. She wrote that she was married, and had a daughter. Ever since then she sent me a letter every Christmas and every Easter with a few hundred drachmas inside. The only thing she asked was that we should never ever write to her. Except if something happened to Fotos.

ELENI

We need to explain things to Roula. She doesn't understand. That's why she's being strange. When she knows, and understands, then she'll feel that she belongs, more. Mother is going to have to tell her now... carefully, though...

We sent for the priest to read a prayer to put Fotos at rest. The priest had no idea what it was really all about... He said the prayer and rested his stole on my brother's head. Three hours later Fotos was up on his feet again, and shouting. Now he's sleeping again.

I have to open the chest now. To get the clothes out so that we can prepare the funeral figures. They'll want airing and ironing, because we haven't had them out since Vasiliki's funeral. She died in 1978, in Giulberi, just outside Larisa.

She had married a Vlach from the Kalarytes. Every summer they used to go up into the Kalarytes with two or three thousand sheep: an entire troop. Families went with children and grandchildren, and dogs and chickens. They used to tie coloured threads to the chickens' feet so that they could tell whose was whose. Vasilo would have one colour, Lambaina another, and Asimina another. They used to set up their tents until it was time to go up Mount Pindus. Then they would do another week on foot, following the animals. They used to winter at Giulberi, and it was there that Vasiliki died. She was the last remaining member of *his* family. I got the news from my sister Despo, who was living in Larisa. We packed up the funeral garments and went. Those Vlachs have some strange habits too. They're a proud race. They talk another language among themselves which we can't understand. Vasiliki was seventy-five when she died. Only Despo and I went to the funeral.

Mother wouldn't even hear of it.

Giulberi was strange. There they lived in cabins made of reeds plastered with mud. They say that it's the women who make the huts. And they're clean as can be. We had to take our shoes off before going in. The floor was covered with rugs, and not a speck of dust in sight.

Vasiliki's husband really worshipped her. A strong old man with a twirling moustache. He wept like a baby at the funeral.

The Vlachs don't have our tradition of funeral figures. But since this was the custom in Vasiliki's family, they went along with it. And they didn't have the tradition in the village either. Maybe in the old days, but not now. . . We were the only ones to keep the custom going. For better or worse. Grandma Maria passed it on to us. Did she bring it here. . .? Or did she find it here. . .? Who knows. Anyway, we keep the custom just as it was passed down to us.

In fact I didn't really go to Giulberi for Vasiliki's sake. I went to look after our garments. In case they didn't look after them as they ought to, and in case they got them all mixed up. These clothes are precious things.

When *his* mother – our grandmother – saw that Despinio was at death's door, she called our mother over. Despinio died young – she was only sixty. This was in 1940, just before the war. Summer of 1940. She had had her confession, and the priest was saying that he would not give her communion unless she first asked my mother's forgiveness. Weeping and sobbing, she murmured words that only Mother understood. Mother nodded to her, as if to say that everything was all right, and that she should be at peace.

'May you be forgiven, dear,' Mother told her. 'It wasn't your fault... that was how they brought you up... let bygones be bygones...'

Later on Despinio told her about the funeral garments: 'You are the only one who can carry on the custom. Grandma Maria passed them on to me. Now you must take them. That is what grandma would have wanted, because she loved you.... Keep them clean and tidy, and may they never be needed – but you must always keep them ready... And I want you to prepare the funeral figures for me when I die...' Those were Despinio's last words. Mother kissed her, and at daybreak she passed away. She had died of a strange illness. Her belly had swollen up like a drum. Mother kept her word. We kept the clothes in a chest that had belonged to grandma. With mothballs, and lavender, and laurel leaves.

ROULA

I don't know what to say...! I mean, when the old lady, my

'grandma', started telling me these weird things, I didn't pay much attention. But then, when she spelled it out for me, I didn't know what to say...! I mean, we're talking serious drama here... Deadly stuff...! Imagine it, that dirty old bastard, wanting to screw his daughter...! Couldn't you just tear the man limb from limb?! My uncle Fotos did well to kill the old bastard... I ask you... The pig! His own daughter...! And then they talk about the purity of the Greek country-side...! And here we're not talking about today, because today it wouldn't have been so surprising – if you want porn, it's in the countryside that you'll find it... No – this was forty years ago. I ask you... My mother...! My mother Archontoula, the sweet, good woman, the pure, decent person...! It's a good thing I don't know where your grave is, you pig, because I'd come and piss on it...! And he never even married the old lady, my grandmother...! Eight children she bore him, and every one of them bastards...! So why did she stay there...? What else could she have done? There she was, a refugee from Smyrna, homeless, and with eight little bastards – where could she have gone? Could she have found a better man...! Probably not. I tell you – men are such wankers – they want hanging up by their dicks, that's what they want. Do you know what he did to my 'grandma' – his woman? First he took her by force, and kept her unmarried all those years, and then he tried to screw his own child, his own daughter... I was raving mad when I found out. It's not that you don't read this kind of thing in the papers... It's just that you don't expect it in your own family... your own mother! ... That's why the poor cow never talked about her family... I'm not surprised she never told me. What could she have said? 'Your grandfather tried to screw me...'?

Just think of it – my poor mum... At the crack of dawn she crept out of the house and ran away... She was so ashamed, she couldn't bear the thought of seeing her mother, and her brothers and sisters. . . Who knows the agonies she must have gone through during her first years in Athens. . .

For God's sake, Mum, why didn't you tell me all this. . .? Why. . .? I would have loved you more. . . What were you afraid of – that I would think badly of you. . .? You could have told me before you died, though. The only thing you said was about Fotos. . .! But you were right to want me to come, because Fotos, your brother. . . killed for you. I must know, Mum – did he get there in time? Did he manage to get his hands on the dirty bastard before he got to you. . .? You must tell me, Mum – did he or didn't he. . .?

MOTHER

Roula is troubled. . . I can feel it. How could she not be? It's a lot for a girl to take in. I spelled it out to her. I began at the beginning. With Vourla, Persephone, Andronikos, and then coming here to grandma Maria's, and *him*, and the children, and *him* trying to lay hands on Archontoula, and then the killing. . . Maybe it will have done her good, because she didn't seem very interested at first, when I told her about my own troubles. But when I started telling her about her mother. . . She went completely wild! She started swearing like I've never even heard a man swear. And she demanded that we show her where his grave is. I told her that we don't know where it is. She started shouting at us, saying that we were trying to hide it. But then she believed us. There, she has lit a cigarette, and she's thinking. . . She's turning it all over in her mind. . . Not that I can see her. . . but I know! I heard her lighter click, and I can smell the smoke, and I can hear her breathing deeply. Let her learn from the pain. . . People who have not known pain in this life don't know what life is.

People who have known pain understand one another...
Those who have known no pain are poor fools. They think
they rule their lives, but it is life that rules them. And life can
turn everything upside down...

My Fotos is taking a long time going. I can see he is in
torment... We called Father Chronis to come and say a
prayer over him, to give him forgiveness and to calm his
spirit, so that he can go in peace... Within three hours Fotos
was up and shouting again... Father Chronis doesn't know
about the sin hanging over Fotos... I shall have to try what
they used to do in Vourla in the old days... When someone
was tormented by a sin and was taking a long time passing on,
they used to bring the person that he'd wronged, to forgive
him... And if the person who had been wronged was dead,
they would place a piece of their clothing on the person who
was about to die... *He* is tormenting my boy, even from
beyond the grave... We hid *his* clothes in a chest in grandma's
old house... I wonder if they're still in one piece, or if the
mice and the moths have eaten them... I shall tell Eleni to go
and look...

    And we have to get the funeral garments out of the trunk.
They need to be aired, and maybe they'll need mending. But
anyway, let's see to Fotos first.

ELENI

Grandma's house is just a ruin now. Full of mice and snakes.
And her husband had built it with such loving care. Right
down to the anchor that he put there. 'So as to remember
Psara and the sea,' as Mother explained. Now the house is a
wreck. The only thing left standing is the anchor.

Look at grandma's room: no ceiling, the windows broken, the beds covered in dust, fallen plaster, mouse droppings... I shall have to search in the chest and see if I can find one of *his* clothes. Anything will do... a jacket, a shirt, a pair of trousers...

The clothes are all covered with dust. And the mice have made a nest in them. Hmm... This jacket will do, although the sleeves are a bit eaten away...

We laid the jacket on top of Fotos when he started shouting. He stopped for a moment... He was breathing heavily... He was rolling his eyes, and opening and closing them. His face looked terrifying... Then he let out a yell and threw the jacket off him... and that was that...!

Since yesterday he seems to be sleeping more peacefully... A really heavy sleep, it is. Our Fotos must be at the gates of the Underworld by now... In a little while his soul will cross the river. That river runs nine times round the Underworld, forming its frontier. Once you've crossed it, you're gone for ever... You can't come back... Your soul travels around its beloved places, for forty days, and then it goes away, to a place in the far distance. If it ever returns, it reappears either in our dreams or in the shape of a moth flitting around the lamps.

I'm tired. My whole life has been tiredness. What pleasures have I ever had? I don't blame Thodoroula's Ritsa for not wanting to learn the mysteries of the Tree. I don't blame her at all. I suppose it's the passing years... I've kept up the custom, with the Tree and its leaves... I see to the funeral garments and the funeral figures. Who would make them up if Mother and I were to die...? You can't have a proper lying-in or a burial without them. These are Fotos's grandfathers and their forefathers before them, who will come to him at his final hour, and who will lead him through to the

Other World and keep him company and teach him the customs.

We have seven garments. Up till now, that is. Because from now on, every first-born son of every first-born son will leave a piece of his clothing to become a funeral garment. Either he will choose it himself, or, if he dies in battle, his family will choose it for him. The first garment we have is from grandmother's captain – Yannis of Psara. He left us a pair of black breeches, a waistcoat, and a red fez... The second garment belonged to the captain's first-born son, Thodoros. They kept the kilt that he wore to the end of his life, and his fine embroidered waistcoat. His first-born son, Yannis, left a gold-embroidered black suit. When they brought him home, he had been dead for two days. According to what grandma Maria told my mother, he was killed in 1904. The fourth garment belonged to my grandfather, Thodoros. He was the father of *him*, the husband of Despinio, who died in Smyrna, in 1922. Despinio chose as his funeral garment a canvas suit, and she sewed onto it the 'Order of Valour' medal that they'd sent her.

The fifth garment belonged to my uncle, Yannis, who was killed in '42. He fell into a German ambush. Together with his wife, Pagona. A wedding suit with a flower in its lapel – that's his garment. It was the only piece of his clothing that we could find. His eldest son, Thodoros, went in '61, and he was hunted down like an animal in the countryside. He grew up an orphan. He got involved in politics somewhere, in '47. At the same time that we lost my brother Yannis. My cousin Thodoros lived through that period without prison or exile. But in '61 some of the opposition movement lay in wait for him, and clubbed him to death. He died on the spot. And he was only forty. He left a widow, and a sixteen-year-old son, Yannis. His wife chose his funeral garment for him – a pair of trousers and a flannel shirt. People were in great poverty in those days. . . She wasn't to be allowed to enjoy her son either, her Yannis. The last garment – the seventh one – is his. A simple shirt. Stained with blood. They took Yannis away in April 1967. A friend of his brought us the shirt secretly in '68. It was wrapped up in a ball. The friend told us that Yannis wanted this shirt to be his funeral garment. So that was what we did.

ROULA

God, these old women are completely barmy! From what my cousin told me – Ritsa, that is – they've got a special tree. They lie down under it, and the tree moves its leaves over them, and they start talking prophecies. I mean – I ask you! In the twentieth century. . . when people are landing on the moon. . .!

Basically, Ritsa and I have decided to help out here as much as we can. We'll put up with all their weirdnesses, so that the poor man can die in peace and we can get back to our jobs. Well, actually Ritsa hasn't really got a job, but now she's met me she's asked if I can help her to go to Athens to see how the other half lives. Because here, well, I mean. . . 'The place that time forgot,' that's how she described it.

OK, Roula, here we go! The crunch has come. Uncle just started calling, 'Archontoula, Archontoula,' and the old lady, my 'grandma', is pushing me gently towards him.

His eyes are shut. His hair is still blond, for all his years. He must have been a good-looking man. . . Why did he have to end up here. . .? He's lifted his head and he's sort of making faces. As if he's talking with someone, but without opening his mouth and without making a sound.

The old lady, my 'grandma', takes my hand and lays it on his hand. I'm getting all emotional. And as he slowly opens his eyes, he looks just like a child... He's calm now. Not trying to get up. Not shouting... Ever since they laid that loathsome man's jacket on him.

I can see that he's looking at me. He must be ever so tired. His eyes light up when they see me, and he opens his mouth a little. 'My Archontoula...'

I'm crying. Silly idiot, I'm crying. It crept up on me, just like that, and I can't help it. Here's this man, and he's dying, and he's got my mother's name on his lips... And when my mother died, her last words were for him too... They got on well together, as brother and sister... What about me, though? Who's going to call *my* name when they die? The old lady, my 'grandma', is stroking my head and whispering in my ear what I have to do. I can't speak. The words come with difficulty...

'My Archontoula...'

'My brother,' I whisper, as the old lady told me to.

'Was I in time?'

That's all he says – 'Was I in time?' I've been wondering exactly the same myself, ever since the old lady told me all those things this morning. I hug him, I kiss him, and I say: 'Yes, my Fotos... Yes, my brother...' I no longer even know what I'm doing... I've fallen into his arms and I'm crying my eyes out and saying: 'Relax now... You can relax now, everything is all right,' and 'You saved me,' and all kinds of things that I don't even know I'm saying...

What on earth came over me...? The old lady – my 'aunt' – took me out into the yard. I thought I was going to faint. She made me sit down, and washed me and moistened my hair with water. She made the sign of the cross over me, and said: 'You granted his wish.' Then she rushed off. 'There's a lot of work to do now.' That's what she said.

MOTHER

Now Fotos can be calm. He can go in peace. My Archontoula's Roula was so good, bless her. It was as if I was hearing the voice of Archontoula herself. Is it possible that she could have been speaking through the mouth of her daughter? Can ordinary people understand these things? No, I'm sure they can't... There is an abyss between us and them. So many mysteries in life... I am the only one who knows how my Persephone was lost... I never told a soul. So how was it possible that my Eleni had that dream where she was lost in the forest for four days...? When she told me about it, my heart leapt into my mouth, but I didn't admit to her that that was how my Persephone had disappeared.

Eleni must have been thirteen at the time, I suppose, when she had her first blood. Was she scared? Did it frighten her...? She ran off into the woods. She stayed there for four days. One evening, she said, she had climbed up a tree to sleep, and she dreamed that she was playing with other girls, and they were gathering flowers in a meadow. There were roses, crocuses and violets, lilies and hyacinths. But the girls were all attracted by a narcissus. From its roots a hundred flowers were sprouting forth, and its sweet scent was all around. Eleni says that she went to cut one of the flowers, but no sooner had she taken it in her hand than the earth opened up. The meadow turned into a sort of hell. A man of rank came rushing by on a chariot which was drawn by green horses with blue manes. My daughter – my Eleni – screamed and screamed, but in vain. The man took her with him and they disappeared into hell.

My Eleni was very frightened... and it was then that she began going to the Tree... And I too was very disturbed by this, because that was just the way my Persephone had disappeared. In a village just outside Kavala.

After the Catastrophe, we went to Chios. There were other people there from Asia Minor too. From Smyrna, and Aidine. We were living in some olive oil warehouses. I didn't know any better, and soon sold what little gold I had. The only thing I had kept was Persephone's gold baptismal cross. And in the end I had to sell that too, to the captain of a caique, to get us to Kavala. Andronikos had relations there. Two sisters. We weren't welcome in Chios, you see. The local people used to abuse us, calling us 'refugees' and so on.

And when things began to get very difficult, Persephone suddenly started bringing bits of food home. Sometimes a piece of bread, sometimes a few sprats. I realized that my daughter had been out begging...! No, I said to myself, it would be better to take a boat and go to Kavala. It couldn't be worse than here... But it was ... My in-laws chased me from their door. So we had to move on again... We would settle wherever we happened to find work. We stopped again, in a village just outside Kavala. The boss said that I could have work until winter. All the women workers and their children had to sleep in the sheds where they stored the tobacco. The place stank of saltpetre, but what could we do? The boss fed us, too. Bread and cheese at noon, and in the evening tomatoes and rice, bulgur and suchlike. He kept some of our money back for the children. We would have gone somewhere else if we could. While we were working in the fields, the children used to play nearby. One day Persephone was playing with her top, and she saw this wonderful flower, a narcissus. That was what the other girls, her friends, told me... How was it that my child disappeared...? Who knows ...? She must have got lost somehow and been unable to find her way back. That was what I thought at the time, and so I took to the road, to look for her.

When Eleni told me of her dream, I thought, 'My Persephone's gone, now, she's lost for ever.' That was what the dream revealed to me. But I didn't believe it. Nor do I believe it now. Who knows...? And then there's the little cross on Eleni's shoulder... Just the same as Persephone's cross... identical...!

ELENI

Why is Mother standing there like that...? Is she dreaming...? We have work to do here... I called the priest, to give our Fotos communion. Fotos is on his way out... He probably won't last the night... And mother is dreaming... I sent Ritsa to fetch the priest. Thodoroula will telephone our brothers and sisters in Larisa. I have to cut canes for the funeral figures. I mustn't expect anything from Roula now. The girl is upset. The way her voice sounded – it was exactly Archontoula's. Holy Archangel, deliver us from our sins...!

The priest stayed with Fotos for an hour. I wonder whether Fotos confessed and told him... Who knows...! I watched the priest's face as he was coming out, but I couldn't really tell. Did he know... or didn't he...?

Fotos is ready now. He has received the sacrament. He will die strengthened by the Holy Mysteries. He is ready for the great journey. I wonder which road he will take... How will they judge our Fotos...? Will the spirits torment him, or will he be forgiven so that he can go to Paradise...? Who can tell...?

Our pomegranates are all large and red. I shall choose the largest of them. Seven. And a handful of dry wheatstalks. They have to be tied together with red thread. Where the two canes form a cross. I have to air the clothes, and iron them, and see if they need sewing. I shan't wait for Thodoroula. I'll make a start, and she can help me when she comes. But what is Mother doing. . .? Why does she keep rummaging through that drawer all the time. . . Leave her be, I'll find out what she wants later.

The chest belonged to grandma Maria. It's a handsome chest, made of walnut. The only thing we put in it is the clothes for the funeral garments. Nothing else. We store them with mothballs.

It's not here. . .! I've taken them all out, and sorted them, and shaken them, and I can't find it anywhere. . .! It can't have got confused with some other shirt, because there's no mistaking it. . . It's covered in blood. . .! But how can it be missing. . .? After Vasiliki's funeral, Despo was with me and we gathered them up and put them into the chest. And they were all there. . . So how can it be missing now. . .? It's a bad omen. . . I won't tell Mother yet. . . I'll have another look. . . And I'll wait for my sisters too. . . Oh, I can't even bear to think of it. . . What happens if we can't find it. . .? Mother, Mother, evil has fallen upon us in the vale of our lives. . .!

ROULA

These old women are completely out to lunch. My 'grandma' made me sit down and write a letter to another of her daughters, called Persephone. She told me to write: 'As soon as you get this letter, THERE where you are. . .' (She wanted me to write the 'there' in capital letters) 'give me a sign at once.' Fine, I thought, so she wants to write to one of her daughters... No problem. But then she told me that she was going to put the letter in my uncle's coffin so that he could give it to her daughter in the Other World... I mean to say, what is all this...?! OK, my uncle's dying. You can see it. He's fading fast. I don't know much about these things, but even I can see it. This is the first time I've seen anyone start a correspondence with the dead though! Anyway, she doesn't even know if this daughter, Persephone, really is dead. She's 'lost', she says. But since she hasn't found her in sixty years of looking, she's decided to send her a letter! And what about the other old lady, my 'aunt'... Holy Mother in heaven, where've you sent me?! She's been making crosses out of bamboo canes. Big crosses, the height of a man. Where they join together she's fixed a pomegranate and some stalks of corn, and now she's dressing them with clothes that she's fetched out of an old trunk. She's put a pair of black trousers on that one, and a waistcoat, and now she's sticking a fez on top. It looks like a scarecrow...! She must be planning to make seven of these scarecrows, because she's made seven crosses. I'm keeping out of the way! I'm not going to encourage them, because they'll only want me to join in. The trouble is, ever since they saw me crying over my uncle, they've started sweet-talking me. They seem to think I've become one of them. But I was crying for different reasons. For my *own* reasons, for God's sake! Come on, let's get this over with, because I've had enough of this dump.

MOTHER

We dressed my Fotos in wedding clothes. He went as

peacefully as a bird. He took a couple of breaths, gave a little sigh, and went. Just like that! Eleni tells me that at about eight, which was when he passed away, she saw a moth flying round the lamp. All my children were here. Eleni closed his eyes and kissed him. I asked her to. We dressed him in wedding clothes. And I made him a wedding chaplet out of cotton wool, tied with red cotton. I told them not to cut the calico with scissors. I took it, folded it in four, and gave it to them to burn the point. Then I tore it with my own hands. My Eleni, my Thodoroula, and Despo dressed him for me. I told them to be careful not to put black socks on him, because they make the bones go black. And I gave them *kremezi* to boil...

It's finished. And I'm finished too. I'm empty. I can't even cry. How can that be...? If you open my innards, all you will see is black... And I cannot weep. It won't be long before I go to meet my Fotos. What a son, what a warrior...! How he always stood by me! He was the man of our house. Our prop and mainstay. *He* was our support...! We expected everything from him. He was the one who cleared the filth from our house... My Fotos vowed to remain single, just so that he could look after Eleni and me. He would do absolutely anything for me. And for his brothers and sisters too. Anything...! And now I cannot find the tears to weep for him...

It will only be us at the watch tonight. My daughters and my granddaughters. We don't want outsiders. The table will be set, and plates will be laid out for our elders, and Fotos's plate too. We shall all eat together. We shall fill Fotos's plate and glass, for the last time...! We shall also put food on the seven plates before the funeral figures. And if the elders are willing, Eleni will speak with them. I would like it to happen... for my Fotos's sake...! It would be good for my

Fotos... It would show him that they love him, and want him to be by their side. I placed the candle in his mouth. I myself made it, from wax, in the form of a cross, with a little bit of incense inside. In his hands I placed his hoe, and the letter for Persephone. I've lost hope of ever finding her in This World. And if she is on the other side, my Fotos will find her... Fotos would do anything for me... He will search among the shades, on the other side of the freezing black river. There in the meadows of asphodel, where the souls live, hidden from our eyes, wearing purple robes and walking among the grey flowers. In the salty pastures that border the Mediterranean. Ah, my sea! How much I have missed you! Where are you, my Asia Minor? My Promised Land...! I have lost beauty itself... I have forgotten what beauty is...! I have only ever had time for the necessities of life. Bread, milk, the children. Oh! It's been so many years since I saw the sea...! And plunged my head into it. And let my hair float like the seaweed. The beauty has gone out of my life. Now I understand it. I have been tied to a wheel, going endlessly round and round. Looking after the children, the sheep, the fields. All work and worry... The best years of my life passed in an instant. When Andronikos's proud head reddened the sea. Jealous sea...! You took him from me...! Oh, if only I could dive in and go searching for him...! And my Fotos is – oh, soon I shall be saying *was* – beautiful. I remember him at fourteen years of age, when he began to grow hair in his armpits and round his sex. Up until then we all used to wash in the barrel, taking it in turns. But one day – I remember it, it was the eve of Palm Sunday – Tassos, the scamp, said: 'Look, Fotos's willy has grown.' Fotos fled, and from that day on he used to go and wash in the stream. Like a god, he was...! Blond, blue-eyed, beautiful...!

Your beauty, your goodness, your manliness, my Fotos...!

Where shall I find the likes of you again. . .? I think that either tomorrow or the day after the door will open, and you will go in. . . Poor wretch that I am. It hasn't yet sunk in that he's going, that he has come to the end. . .! Listen to me carefully, son, because I know that your spirit is fluttering around me. As you go to the place where you are going, you will be accompanied by the funeral figures of your elders, and you will come to two streams. You must go to the right, do you hear. . .? So that you do not forget us. . .! Don't let anybody fool you into drinking from the left one, the one with the white cypress tree. . .! You will be lost for ever. . .! You will forget us, and you won't come to see us. Fotos, for the first time in your life you are going to see the sea. May you love it. May you sit there, on the shore, and talk with the waves. The sea is beautiful!

ELENI

Mother is saying her farewells in her own way. She is saying things out loud, thinking that she is only thinking them. We can all hear her – my sisters and myself, that is. We sent Tassos and his daughters away. Mother is right when she says that she can't weep. We can't weep either. Deep pain is dumb and has no voice. We have our black clothes ready. And anyway Mother and I have worn black ever since Yannis died. I haven't yet told her about the missing seventh garment. I have one last hope. Despo's husband is looking for it at Giulberi. He'll be back in two hours. What will happen if it can't be found. . .? The burial won't be able to go ahead. . . If Yannis hadn't left any clothing behind, then maybe. . . But his last wish was that his bloodstained shirt should be his garment. . . Without that shirt, there can be no seventh garment. And Yannis will stand in the way of our brother. He will block him. He won't let him make his way into the Other World. He will force him to wander like an unjust curse and to beg to be allowed to pass through the Gate... And they, spurred on by Yannis, won't let him pass. Because Yannis will be angry that his garment has been lost. Because his garment isn't just an old piece of clothing. It is his whole life. That's what Yannis will be thinking – how could you lose my whole life...? 'Is that how little you thought of me...?' he will say. And he will get even more angry...! No, no, whatever happens we must find the seventh garment.

The other six are all beautifully arranged, with their pomegranates and their stalks of corn. It is as if our elders are standing right there before us. Captain Yannis with his breeches; old man Thodoros with his kilt; Captain Yannis with his black uniform; grandfather Thodoros with his drill suit and the medal on his chest; my uncle Yannis with his wedding suit; my cousin Thodoros with his working clothes... And only Yannis, my nephew, is missing... Where is his bloodstained shirt...? We have one cane cross, with its pomegranate and its corn stalks, standing bare. Holy Mother of God, make it so that the seventh garment is found! Otherwise a great evil will fall upon us.

We have everything ready for the nightwatch. The candles are burning at Fotos's head and feet. The plates are ready on the table. We carried the table into Fotos's room. That's where we shall have the funeral supper. For the last time we shall lay his plate and glass. We shall watch his glass all the time, to see whether his spirit comes and drinks from it. And we shall set plates and glasses before the other funeral garments too. This is how we have always done it. This is how we make them well-disposed to receive the dead person in their midst, and to guide him through the nether regions.

Thodoroula has been cooking rice. She has given a plate to Roula too.

ROULA

Uncle is on his way. May God have mercy on him. Tomorrow it will be the funeral. They certainly do things differently here. They keep the body at home until the time comes for the funeral. I'm not looking forward to it – the old women will be weeping and wailing all night. Oh well, I suppose I'll have to put up with it. And tomorrow morning, as soon as the funeral's over, you won't see Roula for dust... I'll be gone!

It's uncivilized, keeping dead bodies in the house. In Athens everything's done much more tidily... You call the undertakers, tell them where to come, and they take care of everything for you. They take the body away, and you don't see it again till the funeral. Or rather, half an hour before, in the funeral chapel. The undertaker arranges the gravediggers, and even the coffee and brandy afterwards – everything. All you do is pay. I can see I'm in for a hard time here. Apparently they sit up all night keeping the dead person company. I mean to say... OK, the old man's dead, but that doesn't mean we have to sit up crying all night. Not to mention the fact that we all have to sit and eat a meal next to the corpse. This is necrophilia...! I mean, these old women are really something else. They want locking away. The world's speeding by outside, and they're still plodding along like donkeys. Ritsa's right when she says she wants out. When the time comes, she can come to my place and I'll see what I can sort out for her. We seem to like the same things, so we ought to get on well together. I tell you, it's just as well that there's the TV nowadays for country people to know what's going on in the outside world – Ritsa knows about pop stars, and world politicians, and all that. How would she have found out about all that without a TV...? Maybe she can get a job in a factory, or in a store somewhere. Better than mouldering away in a creepy dump like this. And get herself a boyfriend and have a bit of nooky. I'll have to tell her the facts of life, though, so she doesn't end up in the same mess that I did. We won't say a word to the family, not till the last minute. And what will they do with her – shut her up in a convent? Cool it... That kind of thing's over now. Finished. Women's liberation, my friend...! Our bodies are our own, as the feminists say. And I've got the message loud and clear. Mind you, when women go on about being exploited, I say why can't they just let people enjoy themselves? 'Make love, not war,' as my friend Makis says, and quite right too!

I mean, Ritsa's pretty shrewd. She explained to me all about the clothes. They don't hang just any old clothes on the canes. Their ancestors left all those pieces of clothing specially, and if they happened to die in battle, then their families chose them. She says that there are clothes here dating back to 1821 and even before. Every time there's a funeral, they get them out and set them up. But it's only the first-born son of a family that can leave a funeral garment. And then his first-born son after him, and so on. They have seven funeral garments here. They begin with a Captain Yannis from Psara, although God knows what the poor devil was doing here in Thessaly, seeing that he came from Psara.

The old lady, my 'aunt' (Eleni, I mean, because other 'aunts' have turned up as well – Ritsa's mother, Thodoroula, and another one, called Despo, from Larisa – all of them my mother's sisters – and one brother, called Tassos) has been rushing round like a lunatic. She says she's lost the seventh funeral garment. A shirt. And she says that they'll be in big trouble without it. I told Ritsa to put another piece of clothing in, to get it over with. But Ritsa says that it's impossible, because the other one was bloodstained.

It's amazing, the weird things that go on in families! And you can't even switch a light on to see what's happening, because they haven't got electricity. We're going to have to do everything with candles and oil lamps. The whole place smells of incense, and it's giving me the creeps. I can't wait to get back to civilization...

MOTHER

This is a disaster...! A funeral garment lost...! This has never happened before. My boy's shirt has gone...! His blood-stained shirt...! A great catastrophe will fall upon us. It *must* be found! It can't just be lost like that... It can't just have vanished. It's an insult to the dead person, to our Yannis! He will be angry...! He will let loose the wrath of nature, and he will never allow my boy, my Fotos, to find rest. No...! But we cannot have the funeral without the seventh garment...! Despo's husband came back from Giulberi and said that he couldn't find it there. So they'll all have to go out and search... search, and ask.

Yannis will be angry...! Why, my brave one...? It's not our fault. Didn't we keep your garment, as you asked us to...? Didn't we honour and respect it...? Have pity on my boy, my Fotos...! Would you leave him unburied...? Don't you know that an unburied body torments the whole country...? The whole town...? The whole world around...? Raging winds will rise, the waves will become mountains, and boats will sink and men will drown... Storms will howl, roofs will be blown off, and babies will die at their mothers' breasts.

Voices and loud noises in the night will drive people mad. . .
And other voices, mysterious voices, will make women run
into the forest and will send them mad, and they will eat their
own children. No, my Yannis, don't do that to us. Don't hide
your shirt from us. How can we bury Fotos without the
seventh garment? What you are inflicting on us is a terrible
punishment. Instead of being able to mourn our dead Fotos,
instead of sitting down to eat with him, and keeping him
company for the last time, we are all worrying about your
garment. . .! His sisters have all gone out, searching everywhere, to find your bloodstained shirt. . . And instead of
cradling my son in my arms for the last time, I am here,
falling on my knees and pleading with you.

You, Captain Yannis - can't you tell him something?
Didn't I look after grandma, your wife, better than a
daughter. . .? Did you have any complaints. . .? No. . .! Tell
him. . . You are the first of our family line. . . Say something to
Yannis. He's right to be bitter. . .! I know that it was unjust
that he should have died at the age of only twenty.
Treacherously hit from behind. But why has he only got
angry *now*. . .? Why did he go to the funerals of the others. . .?

It's not my Fotos's fault, I know it isn't. It's the times we
live in that are to blame. The world is going to the dogs -
that's the reason. Yannis says that it was unjust that he had to
die. . . Nobody ever thinks of *my* sacrifices, though. People
are only interested in lining their own pockets. . . Nobody
thinks any more. . .! God gave them the brains of humans, but
they think like animals. Yes, Yannis, of course, you're
right. . .! But why choose the moment they bury Fotos. . .?
Isn't it enough that he had a whole life of torment? Do you
want him to stay unburied, to wander the world for ever,
without ever finding rest. . .?

Yannis, I am an old woman, and blind. I live far away from
the world. What did I have that I haven't lost. . .! A fine

husband, the sweetest imaginable; a daughter like the cool waters of a stream; a beautiful house; a country that was a garden of Eden. . . And I lost it all. . . What haven't I suffered in my life. . .? An evil man found me, and kept me by force; he left me unmarried, and never even cared for his children. . . I too have known suffering, Yannis. I understand you. You died for something good. But where is it now, you ask. . . Why don't people understand. . .? In a while they'll be back walking on all fours again. . .

I'm tired. How can I persuade you, Yannis, my child. . .? You're right too. . . I can do no more. . . I shall sit next to my first-born son. Next to the dead man. I shall send for my daughters and granddaughters. We shall do the funeral supper in the proper way. We shall spend the night awake with Fotos, as is his right. Can't you forget your anger, my Yannis, and help us to find your bloodstained shirt. . .? The funeral has been arranged for tomorrow morning.

ELENI

We put rice on all the plates – the plates in front of the funeral figures and those on the table. Seven plates in front of the funeral figures, and seven on the table. We sat down, with Mother at one end of the table and Fotos's empty place at the other. There's Thodoroula, Despo, Roula, Ritsa and myself. We don't want outsiders. Not even our brother's wife. Only the women will keep the night watch. We placed a plate in front of Yannis's unclothed funeral figure too. Let's hope that the shirt is found by the time of the funeral. . .

Fotos's plate is filled for the last time. There is water in his glass, so that his soul can drink, and refresh itself. My brother must be scared now. Because he knows that without the seventh garment there can be no funeral...

The water in Fotos's glass moved. We all saw it and we fell silent. Fotos was drinking. Mother saw it too, and she crossed herself. It's strange – we aren't crying tonight. Mother isn't weeping and wailing. Tonight we shall talk together. We shall remember our childhood years. We shall talk of Fotos and the good man that he was.

It's cold. There's damp in the air. All the doors and windows are open, in case his spirit gets trapped inside the house. I know what Mother wants... She told me earlier... She wants me to call up the spirits of our elders to speak. Because their spirits are all around us; you can feel it. Even Roula and Ritsa, who don't know about these things, feel it. I don't know if I'll be up to it... My mind's all over the place... Maybe later... Let's give the elders time to get used to us... We've done this on other occasions, but only once did they agree to speak. I fell ill afterwards. I was completely exhausted for three days.

Mother is telling stories about Fotos. She says that when he was very young Fotos strangled two snakes with his bare hands. He was holding them, and he was laughing, not understanding how dangerous they were... Now she will tell the other story, about the tortoise shell. She always tells the one after the other. Fotos took it into his head to stretch some sheep's gut across an empty tortoise shell, and to make something that would give off musical sounds. He more or less managed it, but it didn't sound very good, really...

This vigil isn't going like others we've had. We're all worrying about the shirt. And Roula won't sit still either. She keeps getting up and going to the door. As if she's too hot, but it's cold in here. I have to prepare myself. I have to try. It would be good for Fotos if our elders were to speak...

ROULA

I'm hanging on by the skin of my teeth, here. It's like something out of a thriller! There are the scarecrows, dressed in those clothes, leaning against the wall, with a plate of rice and a glass of water in front of each of them. And on the table there's the dead man's plate and glass too. Scary stuff. . .! And all of a sudden the water in my uncle's glass moved. I saw it. It really did happen. Maybe someone moved the table, or maybe there was a draught, I don't know. . . They've got all the windows open too. . . I have to admit, I'm scared. We don't have things like this in Athens. Anyway, I'm stuck here now. . . And it wouldn't do for me to show that I'm scared. . . That's why I keep wandering to the door. I feel like I'm suffocating in here. . . the rice isn't suppose to be eaten – not that it matters, because I wasn't feeling hungry anyway. . . Just now my 'aunt', Despo, brought in a jug with some sort of black juice in it – *kremezi* they call it. It would make you sick just to look at the stuff, let alone drink it. But she says that I have to. First because it's a tonic, and second to show that we're in mourning. It's all 'you must' and 'this is the way we do things' and 'that's our custom'! That's why they live like stupid peasants all their lives, with their oil lamps and their dead people's clothes. . .

Now the old lady, my 'grandma', wants my 'aunt' to get the dead to speak. God, it sends shivers down your spine. . . Not that I believe in all that. Anyway, my 'aunt' has started doing weird things. First of all, she washed her face at the table. Then she let her hair down, and settled herself into a chair and drank some of the black juice. She's opening and closing her mouth, and her eyes are shut, and she's rocking to and fro. The old lady, my 'grandma', keeps repeating some weird word and knocking on the table with one finger. It sounds like a heartbeat. My 'aunt' is sweating. She's twisting her head around, and breathing heavily. God – I can't stand this – I'm leaving... Oh, dear God... There's an old man's voice coming out of my aunt's mouth...!

ELENI

'We bring you greetings! We are all here. I, Captain Yannis, of Psara, and my first-born son, Thodoros. My first-born son Thodoros, and his first-born son, Yannis. The first-born son of Yannis, Thodoros. The first-born son of Thodoros, Yannis. The first-born son of Yannis, Thodoros. The first-born son of Thodoros, Yannis. Seven generations.'

MOTHER

My Eleni is tired. But it was good that grandma's husband spoke. He spoke for all of them. A quiet man, even though he was a sea-dog and a warrior in his youth.

One day, long ago, there was a wedding in Psara. Maria had gone with her parents. It was there that she met Yannis, her captain, properly, for the first time. Yannis was in the company of a softly spoken fair-haired young man. He was travelling through those parts. He had his mother with him too. She was like the Virgin Mary, grandma used to say. So calm. Grandma had known about Yannis for years. But there, at the wedding party that evening, was the first time she had paid him any attention. She watched the strange fair-haired youth and his mother, laughing and joking as people poured them wine. And because Yannis was sitting next to them, she found herself watching him too. And Yannis didn't take his eyes off her the whole evening. The next day he came to see her parents to ask for her hand, and the next month they were married. They had five children together. They suffered a lot, but they stayed together to the end. . .

Captain Yannis's first-born son, Thodoros, married a woman from Mataranga – Vassilo. I shall tell it as grandma told me, which is how her daughter-in-law Vassilo had told her. They lived here, in Rizes, in grandma's big house. Vasilo bore him two boys. His first-born – Yannis, here – and Spyros. And two girls – Maria and Kontylo. In 1878 Thodoros was fifty-eight years old, and Vassilo was forty-eight. He was ten years older than her. In 1878 they got news that Thodoros's father-in-law was dying. So he and Vassilo set off for Mataranga. He had dressed Vassilo in men's clothes, because in those days the area was under Turkish occupation, and they used to take our women. Their idea was to go down to Larisa, and then to follow the river as closely as they could until they reached Palama and Mataranga. Thodoros was scared for Vassilo, because the Turks were very confident. Our people had been at war with them for years, but that year, 1878, the fighting was at its peak. Here in Rizes there were no Turks. Sometimes they would come to the village below, to collect taxes. But they had never come to grandma's house, because the Turks thought that her captain was mad – if you'll pardon the expression – and the Turks used to see mad people as holy, so they didn't bother them. Anyway, after a lot of effort, the two of them – Thodoros and Vassilo – reached their father's wife's village. The village was on a war footing. The liberation fighters were getting ready for war. At one end of his father-in-law's house was the old man at death's door, and at the other end they were making preparations for battle. The village chief, a wise and brave man, was handing out muskets to his fellow villagers. He had bought them with his own money, and had kept them hidden under the wheat in the barn.

At dawn on the twenty-first of March, Thodoros's father-in-law passed away. They were to have had the funeral that afternoon, but there was no time for the rites, and this is why: The freedom fighters were waiting for the Turks at Magoules, just outside Mataranga. They fought bravely. But then a large battalion of Turks arrived – infantry and cavalry. After the battle, the patriots were obliged to retreat to Mataranga. The Turks followed them into the village. They began burning houses and looting. All of Vasilo's family fled. And Thodoros and Vasilo too. They followed the villagers. They had to flee the village at once, even though they still had the funeral to do. Before they left Mataranga, Zisis, the brother of Thodoros's wife, was killed, and Lambros, the husband of his wife's sister, with his two children in his arms. Vassilo was weeping, and Thodoros had to lead her by the hand. Thodoros fell outside Mataranga. At the Rogozino bridge. He received a bullet straight to the heart. He never felt any pain.

When his father died in Mataranga, Yannis, here, was just twenty-seven, and newly-married. I shall tell it as grandma told me, which is how his wife, Chaido, told it, which is what she was told by Antonis, Lambraina's son. Chaido was twenty years old. She had borne two boys – Thodoros and Giorgis. And one girl, Vasiliki. By now everything was quiet, because it was 1881 and the Turks had left our part of the world. Yannis was with his children, working in the fields with the animals. He regretted the fact that the years were passing so peacefully. When he was young he had wanted to go to war. But his father wouldn't let him. That year – 1904 – some soldiers passed through the village on their way to

Macedonia. They were wearing black uniforms. They were going in stealth, to fight against the Bulgarians. Their leader, Captain Mikis Zezas, was looking for local people to act as guides. Their aim was to reach Macedonia by little-used paths and tracks, because the Turks had Macedonia under their control and they weren't letting Greeks in. Specially not Greeks in uniform. The only thing that Yannis asked from Captain Zezas was that he be allowed to wear the black uniform. This one, here, with its black kilt and the jacket decorated with golden buttons and a cross. Yannis was to lead them out of our region, and towards Kastoria. But he wasn't cut out for heroism. Even though he was only fifty-three. As he was going down a mountain path, he felt a tightening in his chest. Apparently he had difficulty breathing and the pain in his chest became unbearable. He died right there, under a pine tree. Of 'angina', Captain Zezas said. Other people knew Captain Zezas better as Pavlos Melas. Yannis left a message before he died – with Lambraina's Antonis, who was also acting as a guide – saying that they should use his black uniform for his funeral garment. Antonis hoisted him onto his shoulder, and carried him, dead as he was, to Chaido, and told her of his last wish...

Thodoros. Husband of Despinio. Grandfather of my children. The fourth funeral garment. We never found out how he died. He disappeared in Asia Minor, somewhere, in '22. I fled, but he remained there for ever. But since it's not right that he should not have a funeral place here, I shall tell a story about him – not because he doesn't have his own story, but because nobody ever learned it. It's not just a story that I've dreamed up out of my head. I know Thodoros's story because he came from the same part of the world as me... That's why I think I can tell it... Because you used to hear stories like this in Chios, in Kavala, everywhere ...

They were being marched up the mountain four abreast. On both sides of the road there were rotten, stinking corpses. At the springs there were sentries guarding the water. When they saw the running water, the prisoners became even thirstier. They were so tired that they didn't feel hunger, only thirst. They would fall to the ground and try to suck moisture from the grass. They would plead with the Turks: 'For the sake of Allah... Water...' Outside one of the villages the Turks were waiting for them with clubs at the ready. They hit anyone they could lay their hands on. Some died... Then they had to march on... for hours on end. Their mouths were all scabby. If you opened your mouth too much, the scabs would run blood. The Turks would leave them in the sun for hours. By midday more of the prisoners had fallen down and died. All of a sudden Thodoros fell too, face down. The mukhtar hit him across the head. The others fled, and left him there. Shortly before he died, a picture flashed before his eyes – his wife, Despinio, and his children, almost as if in a photograph...

Perhaps it was a bullet that killed him... I don't know... I cannot be certain, but I think he must have suffered a lot before he died.

Yannis, Thodoros's first-born, was the same age as me. He was also the brother of *him*. The only one of *his* whole family who ever did anything for us. He was always good to me, and to the children too. And during the hard years he would always bring us things, without the others knowing. Yannis loved Pagona very much. And Pagona loved him in return. They were from the same village, and they were friends. But they had never dared call each other by their names. Everyone in the village would have realized that they were in love. It was heard in their voices... It showed in their eyes. Pagona was very beautiful. Slim and well-built, with her hair tightly twisted into two plaits. She wore her white headscarf with grace, and would pull it across her mouth. When Pagona laughed, her eyes gently flashed. One time – it was during the 1920 harvest, so Yannis told me – they were working together. This was three years before I came here. Anyway, Pagona was making up the sheaves and Yannis was gathering them up. He told her that he wanted to marry her. For the rest of the day, till evening, she went about frowning, and refused to say either yes or no. She no longer smiled at him as before. When they had loaded the last of the harvest, Pagona stood and stared into the sunset, as if she had forgotten something. The June sun was retreating, across the river, to the west, towards Pindus. Pagona looked into the sunset as if she was seeing it for the first time, or maybe the last time. Her face became radiant, and she turned to Yannis and smiled at him. 'Yes,' she said. That's all. At the time Yannis was twenty-three, and she was twenty. She bore him two children: Thodoros, here, and Despinio. They lived together there for twenty years. I remember how their love for each other seemed to grow as the years went by. They would look for secret places where they could kiss, out of sight of the children, behind doors, in the barn. . . Later on they left the village and went to live in Tyrnavo. Still in love. And they were still together in 1942, in the lorry on their way to plant dynamite. Somebody had betrayed them. The Germans had set a trap for them. Yannis called out 'Pagona', and she called 'My Yannis'. . . And that was how they died. . .

They left Thodoros, Yannis's first-born son, alone. He was neither imprisoned nor sent into exile. But his life was very hard in the village. The local policeman expected him to report every day, to show his face. The priest wouldn't let his wife, Chaido, take communion. He wanted Thodoros to go to confession first. His boy, Yannis, was stoned twice. By relations of Mitsos Giza. For they thought that Thodoros had killed Mitsos in '47. But then there was a trial, and witnesses testified that Thodoros hadn't even been in the area when Mitsos was killed. Who can say. . .? Mitsos had betrayed many villagers. . . If his brothers happened to meet Thodoros in the street they used to make a single gesture – a finger across the throat. . . They had a following among the people of the village. One evening they came and stoned Thodoros's house, and they kept it up all night. They had dogs too, and the dogs were barking. Chaido screamed and held her boy Yannis so tightly that she almost choked him. In 1950, some boys from Mitsos's family caught her son – Yannis, that is – who was five years old at the time, and pulled his trousers off. They forced him to walk in front of the church where he went to school, without trousers. When he finally got home, his cheeks were black with tears and dirt. He shut himself away for a day and a night; when he finally came out, to go to his mother, I saw that he had made his mind up. 'I'll show them,' he said – over and over again. Luckily, he didn't do anything. Thodoros even went to the priest and made confession. 'A clear sky has no fear of lightning,' he used to say. All right, he'd been in the resistance, and he'd provided the guerrillas with a bit of bread and a couple of chickens, but he was a man who never bothered anybody. The priest sent him to do penance for three months, after which he would give him communion. So as to calm Chaido too. The boy – Yannis – was furious about all this. . . But Thodoros, who didn't want to see the boy with his trousers down again, tried to calm things down. 'The boy will grow up,' he used to say, 'and he will understand.'

They finally got him during the grape harvest in '61. He was walking through the vineyards early in the morning when Mitsos's two brothers and his son leapt out of the brambles. The son was grown up now, getting on for fifteen.

It was he who hit him. His uncles held Thodoros, and he hit him with a lump of wood. On the head. Maria's boy Lambros saw them, but he wouldn't report it to the police because he was scared. And there, dead among the brambles, is where his son, Yannis, found him.

Now I shall speak of Thodoros' first-born son, Yannis. The seventh funeral figure. I shall tell what I know myself, and also what his mother, Chaido, told me of what Yannis's friend had told her. He was thirteen years old when he found his father dead in the brambles. His father was right to say that the boy would understand. Yannis was in a raging fury. He was forever saying: 'Dad sold out.' Very early on, he joined a political organization. They used to go by bus to villages out in the countryside, to hold discussions with the villagers. The village policeman was always calling at his house. Yannis ignored it all, but he knew that his card was marked. On the morning of 21 April 1967, they came and arrested him. They put him on board a lorry, together with some others, to take them to Athens. That much I knew for myself. What I shall tell now is what was told to Chaido, his mother, by Giorgis from Larisa, the one who brought Yannis's shirt.

They took him to the Hippodrome Stadium in Athens. Thousands of people. Decent people. People who had never been involved in anything. Men and women, young and old alike. There were some of our own people from Larisa, too. The guards either marched them around, or they kept them just standing there for hours on end. Like cattle.

They were taken to go to the toilet, and were standing in a queue outside. I suppose Yannis must have been confused by what was happening to him, and didn't hear the guard blow his whistle. He stepped a couple of yards out of the line. The guard machine-gunned him from behind. Yannis fell. The others ran across to him. Where he fell he had bloodied the earth of the Hippodrome. He managed to see Giorgis, the man from Larisa, and told him to take the shirt. He died right there, in the arms of that Giorgis. He was the first one killed.

And your shirt *will* be found, my Yannis. Otherwise there can be no funeral.

ROULA

I've about had it up to here! Here we all are, stuck round this table, and the old lady is talking non-stop. And they keep sipping at the wine. All the time. At this rate we'll all end up paralytic. Mind you, maybe it's just as well. . .

Look at that – it's dawn already. . .! We've been sitting here for hours now, freezing, with all the doors and windows open. . .! For heaven's sake. . .! And all those creepy clothes up against the wall looking like ghosts.

How on earth does the old lady manage to remember all this stuff. . .? If you asked me how much I remember of what she's been saying, it would be virtually nothing. Leaving aside the fact that I'm just about falling asleep. I've had enough. I decided I'd go through with it, but it's getting too much. Now everybody's working themselves into a state because they can't find Yannis's shirt. And where on earth do they think they're going to find it. . .? Out of a magic hat? Since we're all sitting round here, who's been looking for the shirt. . .?

Anyway, I said why didn't they just put another shirt in. Maybe they could put a bit of red paint on it so that it looked like blood. . . They almost ate me alive. They were furious. . .! Ritsa kept nudging me, to tell me to shut up. Surely you don't expect me to be scared of five crazy old ladies. . .?

What's going to happen to this place when this is all over, eh...? Tell me, what...? How are we going to become Europeans...? With bloodstained shirts, and old women beating their chests and talking with the dead...? I tell you, they need some sense knocking into their heads... Anyway, I thought the priest was supposed to be coming, for the funeral. Don't tell me – the priest is waiting till you've found the shirt...! I mean to say – this is gruesome!

ELENI

Tassos and the others searched all night. Nothing. Not even with the family of Chaido, his mother... Nowhere. But how can this be? I folded them and put them in the chest with my very own hands. They were right on top, because I put them in, in the right order.

No. Fotos can't be allowed to suffer. I have to think of something... And Yannis – he will be very angry. The night watch is over, and his funeral figure is still unclothed. Mother kept the old custom, and told stories... She spoke of Yannis too... But what's going to happen now...? The priest is going to come soon, with the chorister.

I fell at the priest's feet. I wept, and I tried to explain the problem to him. He was very angry. He said that these aren't Christian customs...! The burial clothes...! Not Christian...? Why not? The people who wore them were Christian, after all...!

He wouldn't hear a word of it. Mother tried talking to him too...

The priest said that he'd never heard the like of it – not wanting to bury a dead person...?

We told him that it wasn't that we didn't *want* to. We wanted to. Really wanted to... But without the seventh garment, we couldn't. It would mean that our Fotos would never find rest...! He would become a lost soul... In torment...!

He said that the best he could do was to come back later. At four in the afternoon. And that was already doing a lot. It was the first time he'd ever done such a thing, and he was only doing it for Fotos. Because he had confessed his sins, and had received forgiveness. And out of consideration for Mother and all she has suffered. Mother has aged very suddenly. She's eighty years old, but up till now you'd never have known it. In the space of one night, though, her eighty years have crept up on her! She has always worn black, but now the black really makes her look her age. She has covered her face too, with black crêpe. She is sitting next to Fotos now. The big, strong woman has become like a little ball of wool.

MOTHER

I have to do something. For my Fotos... My child will be in torment... And he will return to torment the world... For a person to be unburied brings great bad luck...! But it also brings bad luck for someone to be buried contrary to custom – he too will be in torment...! I have to think of something... By four o'clock, the priest said. That will be our last chance.

It sounds like a storm is brewing. Listen to the doors and shutters banging. Don't let them shut them... They mustn't be closed. Eleni will have to hold them open with stones... I know why the winds have blown up. They are angry...! And there will be worse to follow... Tidal waves, earthquakes...!

I have to do something... to placate the dead, and to save the living...

'Oh Lord, this woman who has fallen into the ways of sinfulness, beholding your divinity, comes as a bearer of ointments, and laments as she brings you myrrh for your burial. Saying, Pity me, for night is upon me, dark and moonless, and I am driven to lust and licentiousness.

'Accept the well-spring of my tears, thou who bringest the waters from the sea to the clouds. Incline to the sighs of my heart, thou whose ineffable death did move the heavens. I kiss your immaculate feet. I shall wipe them with the hair of my head. When Eve was in the Garden of Eden at the waning of the day, she heard a noise and she hid, in fear. My all-forgiving Saviour, who will fathom the great number of my sins? Do not overlook your servant, thou who hast untold compassion.'

Yes, I think that this is what must happen... Quietly, though... So that nobody notices...! Right, then...

ROULA

God – that's some wind...! It's picking up the chairs...! The house started swaying to and fro with the wind, so we all came outside. Only the old lady, my 'granny', stayed inside, next to the body. The wind actually uprooted a couple of trees on the mountain opposite, and sent them careering down the slope, and a load of stones and rocks too... The dust is stifling...

The way that wind is blowing, it feels like we're going to take off at any moment...! They're placing stones to keep the doors and windows open. The wind lifted off a few tiles, and one of them just grazed me... My 'aunt' says that it's all because of the unburied body. I don't know what the reason is – all I know is that I've had enough. And how they managed to sweet-talk the priest, I don't know...! He said that four o'clock this afternoon would be their last chance!

What will they do? Is there anything else left to do...? The old lady, my 'grandma', has started singing hymns... Whatever happens now, I'm going to keep well out of the way... I'll wait outside until the priest comes at four. We'll get it over with, and then the husband of my 'aunt' Despo can give me a lift down to Larisa. I'm not staying here another night... It's sending me completely crazy...!

ELENI

I heard her singing the hymns and I didn't know what to make of it. It isn't that she isn't religious... But in her own way... For all that the priests condemned her for the life she led... She was singing one prayer over and over again. Mary Magdalene's prayer to Jesus. And she sang it as well as any chorister. I thought, her mind is going... she can't bear the thought of Fotos's death... She has been through so much...

I sat down next to her and took her hand. It seemed cold... She didn't even realize that I was there. She had leaned her forehead on her left hand, and she was chanting the refrains.

'...I came to thy wedding, Lord, but I have no clothes to wear that I may enter in; shine upon the garment of my soul, O Lightgiver, and save me...'

I thought to rub her hands a little, to warm them... Staying up all night, I thought, and all the emotion, and her being eighty years old...

She pushed my hand away. Weakly. She got up, a bit unsteady on her feet, and all of a sudden started undressing herself...!

I thought, Mother has gone out of her mind, she's going mad...

She took off the crêpe veil, her black jacket, her black shirt – the one that buttons to the throat – and stood there in her vest... the white vest that she wears next to her skin...

It was all red...!

'What have you done?' I screamed. 'What have you done...?'

'I have done what I had to do,' she said, simply. And then she fainted.

I unbuttoned her vest. The blood was fresh and she was still bleeding...!

I froze in my tracks. Mother's body had drawings all over it...! Her whole chest was like a picture.

The drawings were a bit faded. There were leaves, and roses... It was so very strange... This must have been why she always insisted on washing alone!

Between her breasts two cypress trees turned their tops towards each other, as if they were kissing. And right there she had cut a cross, and the blood was still flowing...!

She half opened her eyes. 'Now you know my secret,' she said. 'Put my bloodied vest as the seventh garment. And don't say anything to anyone. Only you and I shall know. And God...!'

THE TREE

I love women. Woman and wild flowers. I love the colours of wild flowers. White, yellow, and purple. These are the colours of the land. In ancient times people painted their statues those colours, and in later times they painted their doors and window frames the same. People don't paint their doors and windows frames any more. Those are the colours of crocuses and anemones, lilies, irises and asphodel. White, yellow, and purple.

Women are suffering greatly again. It is women who write History. They carry the world's great events on their shoulders.

In the old days, the maidens from the distant North would come, and we would talk together. Then came the priestesses, clad in white, with their copper gongs, and garlands in their hair. In their white robes they would lie down and wait and listen for the whispering of my leaves.

They would ask me of things both great and small. And I would tell them. Because I knew. The birds from Libya used to tell me and the snakes from Acherousia; and the Sun, the great lover, and the invisible flowers and the far-off stars and constellations.

Women. We have always loved one another. Even when the big festivals came to an end and the women in white began to dress in black. There is always some woman who arrives up here, all out of breath, to ask me things. And I shall answer. . .

Because I love women, and wild flowers.

The great sufferings of women, and the colours of flowers. White, yellow, and purple.